MW00952750

ONBOARD FOR LOVE

A Billionaire Beach Romance

CAMI CHECKETTS

Birch River Publishing

COPYRIGHT

Onboard for Love: Billionaire Beach Romance

Copyright © 2017 by Camille Checketts

All rights reserved.

No part of this book may be reproduced in any form or by any electronic or mechanical means, including information storage and retrieval systems, without written permission from the author, except for the use of brief quotations in a book review.

DEDICATION

To all of my boys: Phoenix who makes everyone happy, Stockton who was so shocked that vacation isn't fun every minute, Memphis who rocked the flow rider, and Denver who thinks he needs to grow up and leave his momma. I love all of you too much!

INTRODUCTION

The Billionaire Beach Romances have been so much fun to write. I've been able to travel to each of the destinations with my sweetheart so that's made it even better! I used the cruise we took our boys on for spring break as the setting for *Onboard for Love*. We had the best time on our trip and I was able to get a lot of inspiration from my boys and events that happened on the ship. Watching the Coast Guard come retrieve a little boy with appendicitis was heart-wrenching, especially when I found out the mom was left behind. I had to write about it.

Each of the Billionaire Beach Romances is a stand-alone novel, but *Caribbean Rescue, Cozumel Escape,* and *Cancun Getaway* do have characters that carry over from book to book.

I hope you enjoy *Onboard for Love*.

FREE BOOK

Sign up for Cami's newsletter and receive a free ebook copy of *The Feisty One: A Billionaire Bride Pact Romance* here.

CHAPTER ONE

Alicia Noir tried to slow down her eight-year-old son, Preston, so he didn't launch them both into the murky waters of Fort Lauderdale Port. Luckily—or maybe unluckily, she thought with a sympathetic wince—he slammed into a large plexiglass barrier instead. He bounced back and laughed. "Wow. Didn't see that."

"You okay?"

"I'm as tough as Daddy." Preston grinned and then pointed at the massive, white cruise ship. "There it is! It's huge! Oh, this is going to be epic. Dad's the best to plan our first family trip. Where do you think he is?" He tugged at her hand again. "How do we get on? Did you know this boat has a flow rider like the one Uncle Carson took me on? I hope I can do it better than last time. How soon do we get on?"

Alicia could only smile at his exuberance. It was exciting to see, actually. He'd always been a happy little chatterbox, but the past school year had robbed most of his zest for life and she couldn't count how many times she'd prayed for a way to restore it. "We have to wait in line and go through the port authority first."

"I just want to see Dad." His steps slowed as they reached the line. The porter had taken their bags when the taxi from the airport had dropped them off. Now they had to go through a metal detector, then fill out medical releases before they could get their key cards and board the ship.

Alicia pulled in a breath, but regretted it. The port stunk like so many types of rotten garbage that she couldn't distinguish one from the other. Preston wanted to see his dad, but she could go an entire lifetime without running into Trav again and be a happy woman. Okay, that was a lie. She loved seeing Trav, as did every other woman in America who fell for him. She simply couldn't handle being the last in the long line of his other priorities: race car, making money, and his beautiful assistant, Holly—though she wondered how Holly dealt with all the other women Trav dated. Alicia pathetically Googled him several times a week.

Her stomach churned just thinking about him hugging some model or actress. Trav was the most charming, good-looking man she'd ever been around, and though the divorce had been final since shortly after Preston's birth eight years ago, she didn't know that she'd ever heal from loving him. She was finally doing good, dating Duke, a nice cowboy who made her smile and shared her passion for ranching and horses. She couldn't allow herself to be swept into Trav's smile again.

They made it through security quickly, with Preston joking with the security guards just like Trav would've done. Preston took her hand and skipped by her side as they got in the back of a very long line for the key cards.

"You excited?" she asked, though the answer was obvious.

"This is gonna be the best time of my life, Momma! Our first family vacation." He beamed.

Alicia didn't have the heart to tell him they weren't a family. Not with Trav, at least. She and Preston were a family, and Preston and Trav were a family, but not everyone together. But what did an eight-year-old understand about divorce and broken dreams and hearts?

This cruise was Preston's dream and she was going to make the best of it, no matter how terrified she was to spend seven days with Trav. Preston had enough hard issues of his own to deal with. She could make it through seven days with her ex-husband.

"There's my boy!" Trav's voice rang out across the room, and everyone in the line turned. She could already hear the murmurs of, "That's Travis Poulsen."

"Daddy!" Preston dropped his backpack at her feet and flew into Trav's arms. The sight of them together made Alicia feel like she was at Disneyland—truly the happiest moment on earth. She'd seen her two dark-haired boys together in pictures and on television, but never in real life. A smile stretched across her face, but at the same time she wanted to cry at all they'd lost. If only she could keep this moment in her mind always. Trav lifted their son up high, the muscles in his arms bulging. He'd always been lean and fit, but he'd gotten even stronger since she'd seen him last.

They turned her way, and their identical fudge-colored eyes sparkled at her. Preston looked far too much like his dad with the dark brown hair and eyes, smooth, tanned skin, and distinctive full lips. Alicia drew in a breath. All Preston needed was the perfectly trimmed black beard and for his face to mold into the manly lines that Trav had.

Stop! She shouldn't be thinking about how good-looking her ex-husband was right now.

"Mom, I found him!" Preston called out happily.

Trav carried Preston her direction. Their son was growing up. Alicia couldn't have carried him like that, but it looked effortless for Trav.

Her ex-husband's eyes swept over her and he gave her his megawatt smile. It was the same smile he flashed at every woman and every crowd, but she couldn't help but believe that his eyes didn't shine like that for anyone else. Oh my, she was a dumb sap and they hadn't even boarded the boat yet. How was she going to make it through this "family vacation"? Preston deserved this, had been begging for it for years, but it didn't make it any easier on her.

"Ally." Trav said her nickname like she was royalty. He'd always treated her like gold, if you didn't count the cheating—not with a woman, but he'd been married to his car. If he was to be believed, he hadn't physically cheated with his assistant, Holly, but he definitely had emotionally. She wondered if they were a couple now. If so, Holly didn't seem to mind sharing him with models, actresses, and wealthy social climbers.

"It's been too long," Trav said. "You are even more beautiful than the last time I saw you."

Alicia's spine straightened. She looked over his chiseled jawline, straight nose, full lips, that skin any woman would die for, and those dark eyes. She could easily return the compliment, but she wasn't going to be sweet-talked by him and it was smart to start off the week with him knowing that. "I'm sure I'm not half as beautiful as the model you're dating this week—what was her name, Tiffany?"

Trav laughed, but there was no humor in it and his eyes turned chilly, from the warmth of the hot fudge to an iced cappuccino. "You'd think by now you'd be smart enough to know the tabloids are full of it."

"Smart enough to actually be practicing law," she threw back at him. He'd attended law school with her at Stanford in Palo Alto, California. She'd gone on to have a successful real estate law practice in Jackson Hole, Wyoming, close to her family ranch in Alpine. Trav had passed the bar effortlessly, then jumped right back into his car.

"Oh, I don't doubt your book smarts. It's your street smarts that concern me," Trav said. "Don't know a pack of lies when they're thrown right in your face."

"At least it wasn't some woman's chest that was thrown right in my face." The tabloid pictures of him and Holly that had devastated Alicia eight years ago had been of his face planted squarely in her bosom. The image still sickened Alicia, even though she'd seen pictures of him with dozens of other women since then, Tiffany the most recent addition.

A muscle worked in his jaw, but he turned to Preston, who was looking sadly between the two of them. "You ready to get on the boat, bud?"

"Yeah." All the happiness had gone out of their son's voice, like a deflated balloon, and it ripped at Alicia's heart.

She blew out a breath, promising herself that she wouldn't pick fights with Trav. They hadn't been able to solve their issues over the past eight years, mostly because she'd refused to see him or talk to him. Her brother, Carson, graciously accompanied Preston to Trav's races or to make the exchange when Preston had weeks with his dad during school breaks, and of course Holly helped out with anything Trav needed. Alicia's stomach dropped. She forced thoughts of the gorgeous blonde from her mind. This week was about Preston and bringing back his infectious smile.

The past eight years had flown by as she established a successful law practice, ran a ranch with her brother and mom, and attempted to raise a rambunctious boy. Preston was the happiest spot in her life, but she always felt guilt about the lack of time she had to give him. Carson and her mom made up for a lot of what she lacked, but with her mom's recent breast cancer diagnosis, Alicia needed to be there for her, pay her mom back for all the love and service she'd given to her and Preston throughout the years.

Preston had gotten it into his head this past school year that he needed a family vacation like all the other kids his age got to go on, and once he got something in his head, heaven help anyone who stood in his way. Over Christmas, he'd talked his dad into the idea and the trip was booked for all three of them without her say. She'd tried to think of any way out of it, but her son needed to feel like a normal kid, especially when his life was anything but. Alicia worked long hours, and it was her mom and brother who picked Preston up from school and took him to hockey practice. She arranged her schedule so she could be at every game, and only worked late at night on weekdays so they had Saturday and Sunday together. Their life was okay, but she'd do anything to help Preston feel normal and happy. *Anything* apparently included a vacation with her ex.

She glanced over Trav's lithe frame again. He was a bit taller than most NASCAR racers at six-one, and he was all muscle—not thick bodybuilding-type muscles, but lean muscles that she couldn't ignore. She knew how it felt to have those muscles pressed against her, and it was all she could do to not let her brain go there. Eight years was a long time, but the desire for Trav rushed back like she'd been in his arms only yesterday.

Still holding Preston, Trav bent down and swooped up their son's backpack, looping it over his arm, then resting his hand on Alicia's lower back and directing her past the crowds. She hated that he could act so comfortable after all this time. The heat of his hand seared through her thin sundress and she wanted to tell him to stop touching her, but people were snapping pictures with their phones and she was sure their little exchange hadn't gone un-recorded. Another reason she'd distanced herself and tried to protect Preston from this life.

"They've got everything ready for us over here." Trav walked them to a desk, where the forty-something blonde gushed over the "little family" and had them sign a few papers. He finally set Preston down, but their son could never get enough of his dad and stayed glued to his side. Alicia was certain the blonde worker would ask for an autograph, but she stayed professional and just sighed slightly when Trav grinned and thanked her.

They went through a door, up an escalator, and across a ramp, avoiding the crowds. Preferential treatment was such a part of Trav's life that he probably didn't notice anymore. Alicia leaned close to his ear and murmured, "I'd forgotten how everybody kowtows to you."

Trav turned, and she realized she'd made the mistake of leaning too close. His cheek brushed her lips, and the soft, perfect-length facial hair felt so good. She should've jumped away, but her body rebelled against her and she just breathed him in while her lips stayed on his face. He smelled like sunshine and hot-man cologne—musk, amber, and pheromones.

"You're the only one who never kowtowed to me, darlin'."

Alicia pulled back and glanced away from the hurt in his eyes. "Told you I was smart."

He chuckled at that, and his laughter threatened to break through the wall she'd built up over the past eight years. Painful memories pricked at her mind: watching her father die in a race car, and then Trav slipping right into his shoes, with the race car always taking precedence and women clamoring all over him.

She snapped her emotions shut and muttered, "How's the job?"

"Fine." He cocked an eyebrow at her, not even acknowledging the danger aspect. Stupid man who thought he was indestructible.

"It's always fine until it's not." She remembered her dad laid out in the casket, and her breath hitched.

"Did you know there's an ice-skating rink on this boat and a flow rider?" Preston asked excitedly.

Oh, Preston. Bless him. She needed to focus on her boy and the family trip he'd been dreaming of, and not the pain of loving her ex-husband but not being able to be part of his race car life. "Do you think I'll be able to surf?" she asked.

They walked onto deck number four and waited in line to show their key card. Apparently, even Trav's fame didn't get him to the front of this one.

"You, Momma?" Preston giggled. "You only know how to work, exercise, and ride horses."

"What? I can do it."

"No way. Daddy is going to rock at it, though." Preston beamed up at his father like he was the best thing since horseshoes.

Island music played and cruise staff danced around them, but Alicia couldn't see much past Trav's handsome face. "Thanks, bud, but just because I'm a world-renowned athlete doesn't mean I excel at every sport." He winked at Alicia.

She rolled her eyes. "Tough stuff, sitting your butt in a car and pressing on the gas."

Trav smiled lazily. "Almost as tough as staying in the saddle."

"You wish," she shot back.

"I wish I could watch your butt in the saddle? Yeah, I do."

"Don't you start with your flirtations and inappropriate comments. I'm not one of your model girls without a brain who thinks everything you say is cute."

"Mom, Dad!" Preston yelled. "Please, stop!"

They both looked down, and Alicia felt her face flame when she realized the crowd around them was again taking pictures. One good thing was they'd be on the ship in international waters soon and she didn't have an international plan on her phone. Maybe by the time she could check the news again and went to a grocery store next week back in Jackson, all of the publicity she and Trav were getting would have died down.

"Sorry, bud." Trav ruffled the boy's hair. "I haven't seen your mom in so long, there's just a lot to talk about."

Alicia's chest tightened. It had been her choice to not see him, but she didn't need it rubbed in her face.

"Sounded like fighting to me, not talking. I'd get a time-out if I talked to somebody like that."

"I'd take a time-out with your momma," Trav whispered so only she could hear.

She shot him a warning look. He needed to stop or she'd be throwing herself overboard or into his arms before day one was over. And she couldn't decide which was worse. Good criminy, she was weak when it came to Travis Poulsen.

They shuffled to the front of the line and swiped their cruise cards, then were gestured along the deck. The employees didn't recognize Trav, and as Alicia read their name cards she realized none of them were from America, so that was probably why.

"What language are all these people speaking?" Preston asked.

Alicia smiled. "Lots of different languages. Cool, huh?"

"I can't understand anybody."

Maybe this week they wouldn't be bombarded with Trav's fans. That would be a bonus to going on a cruise, although she was sure there would be a lot of Americans on the ship.

"Shall we drop your mom's purse and your backpack off at the room, then go explore?" Trav asked Preston.

"Sure!" Preston had already forgotten about them fighting.

Trav gestured them through a door and toward the bank of glass elevators, following slightly behind Preston and Alicia. Preston pressed his face to the wall and gazed out as they rose up.

Trav nudged her. "I'm sorry," he whispered. "Let's try to get along." He nodded toward Preston.

Alicia returned the nod. "For Preston," she whispered. She would do anything for her boy, even if it meant spending the next seven days with the man she'd been running from for the past eight years.

CHAPTER TWO

Trav felt the muscles bunching in his neck as they walked down a short hallway and he used his key card to open the suite door. How was he going to get through the next seven days? Eight years of praying Alicia would forgive him for something he never did, and still nothing had changed—she was as beautiful, appealing, and hard-hearted as ever. Her brownish-golden hair hung down her back like a curtain. He wanted to part that curtain and kiss the soft skin of her neck. Good crap, he was pathetic.

He swung the door wide and gestured them inside. Alicia walked stiffly in front of him. He caught a whiff of her light floral scent and closed his eyes to savor it. Still the same after all these years, and he loved it.

Preston whooped and took off, exploring the rooms. There was a large main area with a wet bar, couches, and a flat screen television; a huge balcony that looked out over the port of Fort Lauderdale; and then three bedrooms beyond, each with its own bath and connection to the balcony. Just what his personal secretary, Holly, had been instructed to book.

"How cozy," Alicia muttered.

"What's that supposed to mean?" he asked, gritting his teeth. Hadn't he just said in the elevator that they should cease fighting?

"Your email from your assistant said I would have my own room."

"You do have your own room. Take your pick." He gestured around. The suite wasn't massive, but there was plenty of space, and if she was complaining, she should see how teeny most of the rooms on a cruise ship were. He'd looked through the website and thought the three-bedroom suite was their best choice. They'd booked too late to secure one of the penthouses, but this was fine. The Alicia he'd remembered was as comfortable mucking out a horse stall as she was battling in the courtroom in a pencil skirt. Had she turned into a snooty brat over the past eight years? He supposed anything could happen in that length of time.

"I don't want to be in this close of quarters with you."

Trav eyed her up and down. She squirmed and tossed that beautiful mane of hair. Then she made the mistake of folding her arms under her chest, and his mouth went dry. Did she think it was funny to torture him?

He took slow, deliberate steps closer to her. She backed away until she hit the wall. Trav rested his arm on the wall next to her and let his gaze travel over the smooth skin of her face, coming to rest on those bewitching green eyes. "Afraid you won't be able to resist me, darlin'?"

Alicia's cheeks went pink. Trav had forgotten about how beautiful she looked when she blushed.

"Mom, Dad! Come check out the balcony," Preston called.

Trav brushed his fingers along the smooth skin of her cheek. "We'll talk about this later, when he's asleep."

"He'll be sleeping with me to preserve my virtue." Alicia ducked underneath his arm.

"I got him his own room for a reason," Trav said to her back.

Alicia glanced back at him, her eyes sparking fire. "You just remember why I came on this vacation—only for Preston."

She hurried out onto the balcony and started gushing over how high up they were, chatting happily with their son. *Their* son. Sadly, Preston was the only thing they shared anymore. Trav joined them on the balcony and just breathed it all in. The view of the inlet and ocean beyond was nothing compared to his family. Most people probably assumed that if he prayed for miracles it had to do with winning races, but lately this was what he prayed for—Alicia and Preston.

Preston turned and grabbed his hand. "Can we go explore? Are you starving? I heard you can eat anything you want on the cruise and they don't even care. Do you think that's really true? Thank you, Dad, for bringing us. Thank you, thank you!"

"You can eat all you want," Trav said. His gut tightened. Was Alicia monitoring Preston's eating? The kid was thickset, but he was active and definitely not overweight. A worse thought hit him. She was too busy working and Preston was home alone without much food in the house.

He focused in on Alicia. Her smooth brow wrinkled and she pursed her lips. "Hold up there, cowboy," she said.

Trav couldn't help but chuckle. She used to always call him cowboy when he was getting ahead of himself. He'd missed it. He'd missed her.

"This little man gets plenty to eat, and I'm *not* neglecting him."

Trav exhaled in relief.

"I just love to eat, though, Dad. Granny says I got a hollow leg, but I'm not sure what that means, and she makes me help her cook and clean up and always eat my veggies before ice cream. Nobody's gonna make me clean up this week and I can have all the ice cream I want, right?"

"That's what vacation is all about." Trav ruffled his son's hair and laughed. He could just imagine Alicia's mom, Ivy, training Preston to help out and work hard. That woman was tough as nails. No wonder Preston was so great and easy to please. He wasn't being spoiled, even though he definitely could be. With the money he sent Alicia for child support, and the fact that she was successful all on her own, he knew money was not a problem.

They walked down the hallway and up a flight of stairs to the buffet. Their suite was off the back of the ship, which was a perfect location for a lot of the features. The buffet was close, and the flow rider, rock climbing wall, and mini-golf were just another flight above the buffet. Trav wanted to experience every feature of massive ship with Preston and Alicia. His family. He caught Alicia's gaze over

Preston's head. Okay, so they weren't really a family anymore, but a guy could pretend he had heaven for a week.

The buffet stretched on and on with every variety of food and drink that anyone might crave—Italian, Mexican, Indian, Japanese, Chinese, and a little of various other nationalities as well. Preston's eyes lit up as they grabbed plates and slowly walked through. He grabbed a hot dog, a hamburger, and fries while Trav and Alicia piled on different salads, soups, pastas, and sushi.

A server found them an empty table and took their drink orders. As they settled into eating, Trav thought about how the employees on the ship were from all nationalities and didn't seem to recognize him. Some of the other passengers had murmured his name, but nobody had approached him so far. That was a surprising break. He liked his fans and tried to always be friendly, but right now he wanted to focus on Alicia and Preston.

They ate in silence for a few minutes. Trav felt awkward and not sure where to start. He wanted to have all kinds of intelligent and fun conversations with Alicia and catch up on everything in Preston's life, but as he chewed a bite of salad, he couldn't think of anything but the lamest option. "Tell me about school."

"School sucks," Preston said, then shoved a quarter of a hot dog into his mouth.

"Pres," Alicia reprimanded. "We don't say that word."

Trav looked between the two of them. She hadn't reprimanded him for ragging on school, just for using the word "sucks."

"I thought you did great in school," Trav said, confused this hadn't come up at Christmastime when Preston had stayed with him for two weeks. It was only February, had things changed since he last had Preston with him. But he and Preston had run from activity to activity —Disney World, Harry Potter Land, Gator Land, Kennedy Space Center. Preston had even talked him into doing the Daytona Experience, though Trav kind of liked having a break from his car for the two months.

The only interesting thing he'd noticed in the two weeks was how Preston repeatedly thanked him and told him he loved him, but he was just grateful his boy had such great manners and a big heart. Had he stopped to ask him about school? Preston definitely hadn't volunteered. Now that he thought about it, Preston had been really upset to go back to school after Christmas break, but Trav had selfishly thought that it was because he didn't want to leave him and his mansion in Boca Raton, just north of Fort Lauderdale, Florida.

"He's very smart." Alicia set her fork down and took a sip of her water. "It's simply been a hard year with the teacher expecting a bit more homework than we're used to, and he hasn't connected very well with his teacher."

"Mr. Yates is a butt," Preston explained before dunking a fistful of fries in ketchup and jamming them in his mouth.

"Slow down, bud," Alicia said. "The food's not going anywhere, and please don't call a teacher a butt."

Trav had to hold in a laugh. He hadn't seen Alicia's mom since she ran him off with a shotgun eight years ago, but he knew exactly where Preston would get that expression. Alicia's mom was as country as they came and called it like it was. She'd called Trav "a butt" to his face one time, and instead of being offended he'd just had to laugh. Alicia was much more refined, but still had the Western feel of a cowgirl. It was a perfect combination.

"Well, he is. Granny's the one who said it." Preston looked to Trav with a plea in his dark eyes. "He hates me, Dad, and he's no fun at all, and I heard Momma trying to explain to him on the phone how we make hard work fun by joking and laughing a lot. So the next day at school he was even more mad at me and told me to stop smiling when I was trying to make my friend, Hallie, smile because she was having a bad day."

"Whoa." Trav's gut churned. Who was this Mr. Yates guy, and why on earth hadn't Alicia changed his teacher? He looked to her for guidance in how to respond. They'd always shared a lot of glances and communication without words, and the habit came back quickly.

"I know what you're thinking." She held up a hand. "I wanted to move him classes too, but the principal and ... everyone else we've talked to feels it would make the situation worse. The teacher is a good teacher, but he honestly doesn't have any sense of humor."

"Then pull him out of school, hire a tutor or something like that." Telling a kid not to smile went beyond lacking a sense of humor.

"He needs to learn how to get through hard times, Trav. If we solve his every problem, he'll never learn how to deal with someone who doesn't cave to him when he looks at them with those dark brown eyes or charms them with his sense of humor and undeniable appeal." She blushed and looked down at her plate of barely touched food.

Were they talking about their son, or him? He shook his head. If he asked her that, she would say that he should check his ego at the door or some other cute remark.

Preston was looking at him for some kind of response and he didn't care if he was an indulgent parent, he didn't want his boy to go through hard times.

"I hate to have you be miserable, bud."

"Thanks, Dad," Preston said, glancing down at his demolished plate of food. "Thanks," he repeated. "You're the best." He looked at his mom. "Can I go make myself an ice cream cone?"

"Sure." Alicia smiled at him.

"Thank you, thank you!" Preston bounded out of his seat, a huge grin splitting his face.

Alicia sighed as she watched him go. "It's so good to see him happy."

"What are you talking about? He's always happy." Trav didn't like the feeling he was getting about whatever was going on. Was it only school?

"It's been a tough year. It's not just the teacher. He hasn't really connected with any of the boys in his class. They all like to play video games and he'd rather be playing sports or riding a horse. His best friend, Marcus, is in the other third-grade class, and Marcus made the higher-level hockey team and Preston didn't. It's just ..." She blew out a breath. "There's too much to tell you all of it right now, but he's just had a lot of knockdowns. The previous two years, his teachers have honestly told me that he was their favorite student and how they'd be laughing at a joke together that no one else understood. They'd brag about how Preston would teach the entire class, including the teacher, a better way to do the math problem. Then to end up with 'the butt' this year. It's been hard."

Trav couldn't help but laugh. "I didn't think I'd ever hear you call someone a butt."

"You need to meet this guy to understand."

"I might have to." Trav's fist clenched. He really wanted to give this guy a piece of his mind.

"Don't even think about it. I've tried several times and it hasn't made things any better. He wouldn't be impressed by your legendary fame, your money, your good looks, or your charm."

Trav gazed into her green eyes, losing himself in them. "Are you?"

"Am I what?"

"Impressed by my fame, money, looks, and charm?"

Her mouth parted, then closed. Then she licked her lips and looked down.

Preston arrived with a towering soft ice cream cone. Just before he reached the table, the swirled ice cream tipped off the cone and splatted to the carpet. "Aw, crap," he said.

A server appeared and almost stepped in the pile of ice cream. "Stop," Alicia called out, in time for him to look down, see the mess, and pull his foot back.

"I'm so sorry," Preston said. His bottom lip quivered. "Sorry. I'm so sorry."

Trav's stomach tightened again. Something was really wrong with his boy and he wanted to get to the bottom of it right now. One look at Alicia's face showed she was as concerned as he was.

"It's no worries, mon," the worker said. Trav glanced at his nametag: Drew from Jamaica. "Happens all the time, my friend. By the end of the week, most of the little men get the cone-building down."

"Thank you, sir," Preston said. "I'm sorry." He licked his lips. "Really sorry."

Why did he keep saying sorry over and over again?

Alicia bent down with a couple of cloth napkins and swooped up a big portion of the fallen ice cream.

"Ah, no, me lady," Drew said. "That's me job. You just enjoy your family and we get it cleaned up." He winked at her, then turned to Preston. "And you, my mon, go make another cone."

"Thanks!" Preston cried out, his grin restored.

Drew held his fist out and Preston bumped it. Trav liked this guy, and he liked him calling them a family. He made a mental note to give him an extra tip at the end of the week.

"Dad?" Preston turned to him. "Will you come help me make another cone?"

"Sure thing, bud." Trav followed Preston, glancing back to see Drew cleaning up the spill and chatting with Alicia.

She laughed at something the guy said. Trav knew Drew was just a friendly guy, but he didn't like the jealousy that churned in his gut. He grabbed Preston's hand. His place right now was with his boy, but he wanted to stand between Alicia and any man who looked at her beautiful face.

CHAPTER THREE

I t took Preston fifteen minutes to finish the towering ice cream cone Trav had helped him build. Alicia was able to enjoy the delicious salad and sushi she'd found on the buffet. It was delightful to eat whatever looked good and not have to make it or clean it up. It was less delightful to watch Trav's face as he learned a little bit about Preston's situation, especially knowing there was a lot more she probably should tell him. Preston was doing better, though, so maybe she could just leave it at things being hard at school and with hockey.

It frustrated her that an eight-year-old was already worried about making the elite team. When she was eight she'd been riding horses and happy to play on a little league basketball or softball team, but Preston lived and breathed hockey. She knew she was a prejudiced mom, but he was talented and worked hard. Yet he played goalie and the goalie they'd chosen was the coach's son. How did a kid compete with that? Unless she wanted to drive him into Jackson Hole to play on a different team, he'd just have to make the best of the situation. He'd done a lot of that this year.

Trav didn't understand why she hadn't just insisted they change teachers, and honestly she still was debating on it, but the principal and Preston's therapist had been adamant that it would be more embarrassing for Preston when the other kids questioned him about it, and that was the last thing Preston needed right now.

"Where to now, bud?" Trav asked as they stood and left the buffet, seeing Drew on the way out and getting one more fist bump and friendly smile.

"Let's explore!" Preston bounced with excitement and took off.

Trav hurried after him. "Hey, bud, let's wait for your momma."

"Oh, sorry!" Preston slowed down and extended his hand. "Sorry, Momma! Uncle Carson is trying to teach me about being nice to the ladies, but sometimes I get too excited."

"That's okay, bud. Thanks for waiting." She took his hand, but gasped when Trav came around to her other side and placed his hand on the small of her back. Oh, my. How could she have forgotten how every touch from this man affected her to the core?

They made their way up to the twelfth floor, admiring the view of the kids' pool section with lots of spraying water features in bright colors, two slides, and a lazy river. Heading to the rear of the ship past the arcade and Johnny Rockets, they watched some yachts glide past toward the open ocean, their sail time wasn't until five so their ship was still in port.

Climbing to the thirteenth floor, they checked out the rock climbing wall and flow rider, which weren't operating yet. They played a round of mini-golf, Trav teasing Alicia because she was remarkably horrible at it. She laughed easily with them. Trav found a worker and asked about the climbing wall and flow rider.

"Our complimentary sessions will start at three-thirty, sir." The guy was muscle-bound and smiley. His nametag said Henry from England. Alicia loved his accent.

"Can I book a private time?"

Alicia stiffened. She didn't want Preston to get in the habit of preferential treatment. She'd worked hard to not spoil him monetarily, even though it would've been easy to do. But this was vacation, right?

"Oh yes, sir. When?"

"Do you want to rock climb or do the flow rider?" Trav asked Preston.

"I don't really like high. Can we do the flow rider?"

"Sure." Trav turned to the guy. "We're going to tour the ship and then get our suits on." He looked at his wristwatch. "Two o'clock work okay?"

"Perfect."

Trav thanked him, and they walked past the basketball court and rock climbing wall and down another hallway. There wasn't much else on thirteen besides a running track and the spa.

"Do you want to book a massage or something?" Trav asked Alicia.

"No, thank you, I'd rather be with you two." Her face colored at how that sounded, especially when Trav's easy grin lit his face.

"I'm not going to complain about time with you either, darlin'."

Alicia shook her head. "You know what I meant."

"I hope you meant what I think you meant."

Alicia hurried in front of him and down the stairs. They glanced into a nice and spacious fitness center. "We could take turns working out in the mornings, if you like," she said to Trav.

"Sure. If we're going to be eating ice cream cones every day, I might need that." Trav winked at Preston.

"Whatever, Pops, you're stinking tough."

"What's with this 'Pops'?" Trav asked, his eyes alight with laughter.

Preston ducked his head and muttered, "It's what Ike calls his Dad."

"Cool. I like it."

Preston straightened up and hugged Trav around the middle in a fierce squeeze. "I love you, Dad."

Trav closed his eyes and hugged Preston tight. "I love you too, bud."

Alicia couldn't help but wish these two could be together more, it would probably be exactly what Preston needed. Sadly, it wasn't going to happen.

Preston released him and grabbed his hand. "Can we look at all the pools now?"

"For sure."

"And the ice skating rink? That sounds cool. Oh, and Drew said there was a pizza place."

CHAPTER FOUR

Trav changed quickly into his suit, his mind playing the words over and over again: "I love you, Dad." Preston had told him that many a time, but it just struck him hard right then. It was so heartfelt. He wanted to be the best dad in the world to that kid, but how could he do that if he hardly saw his boy? A stab of pain pierced him. Alicia wasn't being openly confrontational like she had been when she first saw him at the port, but there was more crap between them than a slurry shed could hold. He kept daydreaming about them being a family, but that was all it really was. Maybe he needed to talk to her about more custody time with Preston, but it seemed like his son was dealing with a lot of junk already. Would being displaced from his main home more often be a good thing or a bad thing for him?

Trav forced himself not to worry about it right now. He wanted to enjoy the next seven days, and then maybe he would have a better grip on Alicia's feelings toward him and what Preston's needs and issues were. He threw a T-shirt on and hurried out of his bedroom. Preston was on the couch, clicking through channels on the television and chugging a water bottle. Alicia's door opened and she glided out. Trav had always loved the grace she moved with, testament to years on the saddle. His jaw dropped as he glanced over her blue V-neck swimsuit covered by a long, white lace cover-up. The holes in the lace thing were big enough he could savor every part of the view. Her shape was just as beautiful as it had been when he'd first met her at eighteen. Her dad had been his mentor and idol, elevating him from the dirt track to NASCAR. Trav had a lucky family connection with her dad's pit crew chief, who was still Trav's chief to this day.

"Wow," he managed. "I like your suit."

Alicia's cheeks got a little more color in them. "Thank you. We'd better get going. It's almost two."

He followed her and Preston down their corridor and up the two flights to deck twelve, where Henry was waiting to help them learn to flow ride. He worked with Preston first, and within minutes the kid was a champ at kneeling up on the boogie board, even lifting his hands, and then turning the board from side to side. Preston progressed to the stand-up surfboard, Henry guiding him until he could cut back and forth.

Trav stood by Alicia's side, aching to sling his arm around her trim waist, but holding himself in check.

Preston had only been going about fifteen minutes when he declared, "That was fun, but my legs are getting tired."

"Let's have the lady give her a go," Henry suggested.

Alicia slipped off her cover-up thing, knocking the breath out of Trav as if he'd slammed his car into the wall at Bristol. She high-fived Preston as he passed her. Had her legs always been so smooth and shapely?

Henry grinned at her as she stepped onto the board and then grasped his outstretched hands. The lean muscles in Alicia's legs flexed as she bobbed and shimmied on the board. Guiding her with his hands, Henry had her riding by herself in no time.

Jealousy clawed at Trav's gut as he watched Henry grasp her waist between his meaty paws and direct her how to cut back and forth on the board. Did Alicia think big, burly guys were attractive? Henry looked like he could be a bodybuilder or something. Trav worked hard to stay fit, but he wasn't bulky like that. He couldn't be hulking and still be competitive in his career. But if Alicia was attracted to that, maybe he could bulk up more.

He shook his head. Alicia was just laughing because of the fun experience. He was acting like a mental case, second-guessing every time a guy smiled at his ex-wife. Maybe it was for the best that Alicia had stayed away from him the past eight years. The next seven days might send Trav running for a psychiatrist.

That night, Alicia noticed that Preston was remarkably well-behaved in the dining room, probably because of his dad's undivided attention. He also developed a crush on their assistant waitress, Mayara, a beautiful girl from Brazil. He glanced shyly up at her every time she asked him a question or brought him something. Their waiter, Shakib from Morocco, and the head waiter, Tom from India, both liked Preston and teased with him. When Tom caught Preston spearing his entire steak with his fork and gnawing on the edge of it, he swooped in and cut it up in a few quick slices. They all laughed about it, but Alicia was a little embarrassed she hadn't noticed her son having atrocious manners. It had to be because Trav had been giving her too many significant glances that she tried not to read anything into. Just another reason she'd stayed away from him the past eight years. She was mush when he looked at her with those deep brown eyes. Darn him.

After dinner they put their suits on and tried out each of the pools and hot tubs. In the main pool area there was a huge big screen television with some football game playing.

"Momma! It's the AFC playoffs. Cameron Cruz and Hyde Metcalf are going to take it all, I can feel it."

The game was in the fourth quarter, so they found a warm hot tub to sit in and watched the end of the game. Denver won, much to Preston's delight. Alicia spent the entire hour trying not to notice when Trav's arm or leg would brush against hers under the water. She sat up on the side of the large hot tub to try to get some distance, but his gaze swept over her as warm as any caress. What was he doing to her? You couldn't have a vacation fling with your ex-husband and not royally screw up your life. Things were going well for both of them and

Preston would get through this rough patch and life would be good. No, her life wasn't brilliant or charmed, and no, her heart didn't threaten to beat out of her chest every time her semi-boyfriend, Duke, brushed her leg or looked at her, but that kind of stuff was for fairy tales, and she and Trav were definitely not a fairy tale. They were a runaway train that had already crashed once. Somehow she'd survived that demolition, but another one would be too brutal to even contemplate.

Alicia felt like she'd been praying through NASCAR races her entire life. When her dad was killed and Trav continued racing, stepping into her dad's sponsor and car as well as finding a woman on the side, she knew she'd reached her limit. They'd divorced shortly after. Racing was just in his blood, or so he said. In his blood more than being with his family, apparently. Just like her dad, who had been Trav's mentor since he was a teenager, and honestly her dad hadn't been the best example of putting family first.

As soon as the game was over, Alicia insisted it was bedtime. Preston groaned, but obeyed. They all showered in their own bathrooms. Alicia was tempted to hide out in her room so she didn't have to face Trav again, but bedtime was always special with Preston. No matter how busy their days, they were together at bedtime. She walked through the main area and into Preston's bedroom, stopping just outside the open door. Trav was singing to their son. His deep voice reached out and tugged at her.

Alicia's heart tripped when she realized what he was singing. Trav used to sing it to her. "Do I love you because you're wonderful, or are you wonderful because I love you?"

Did he sing the song to other women, maybe to that Holly girl who was his "assistant"? Alicia's heart thumped painfully.

The song changed to the silly and completely inappropriate "Oh, Mr. Mr. Johnny Verbeck," about a man who ground up everything to make sausages, including a little fat boy. Preston giggled at the song. Neither of them had noticed her yet, and Trav segued into "You Are My Sunshine." She wanted to just keep listening to their interchange, but she couldn't help entering when she heard their son say, "I love you, Dad. Thanks for bringing me on vacation."

"Anything for you, bud," Trav said with a husky voice like he was fighting back tears.

Alicia walked to Preston's bedside. Trav stared at her, his gaze full of longing and delicious promise, but Alicia was going to stay strong. She knew how that longing could fade, how those promises could be battered with a sledgehammer. She bent down and kissed Preston's cheek. "Good night, love."

"Prayers, Momma."

"Okay. Who should say it?"

"My turn." Preston scrambled onto his knees as Trav and Alicia knelt at either side of his bed. Preston grabbed each of their hands, and then Trav reached his hand over toward hers. Alicia knew she should close her eyes and pretend she didn't see it, but her hand had a mind of its own and crossed the distance. Trav's hand covering hers was sure, steady, and it would be her undoing if she let herself dwell on how right it felt.

Preston blessed his horse, his granny, his uncle, his friends, his hockey coach, his momma, and his dad; then he finished with, "And thank you for making us a family again. We love thee. Amen."

Alicia squeaked an amen past her constricting throat. Oh no. One day together and Preston thought they were a family again. It was like a horrible remake of *The Parent Trap*, but real life wasn't a movie. Why she let Trav keep his hand around hers and help her to her feet was beyond her. They both murmured good night to Preston, and then, as if in a dream, she let Trav lead her to the main area, sinking into those deep brown eyes.

"Ally," he murmured. He stepped a bit closer. "Being here with you. Preston's prayer. I feel like ..." His voice lowered. "Could we talk, could there ever be a hope—"

Alicia wrenched her hand free, shaking her head and forcing herself to harden her heart to him. "Please don't do this to me, Trav."

"Don't do what?" His eyes were like a puppy dog now, all appealing and sad.

"We aren't revisiting the past. You and Preston planned this trip and I came along for him. Please respect me enough to not treat me like some twenty-two-year-old who's going to fall at the hot race-car driver's feet."

His jaw hardened. "I've always treated you with respect."

"You have, so please keep it up. We're not playing house this week. I'm not a vacation fling. We'll have a great time for Preston, then we'll go our separate ways again."

He studied her for a few seconds. "You're a fabulous mom, Ally, but maybe you need to do what you want sometimes."

"I've got an amazing son, a successful career, and a family that loves me. What else could I possibly want?"

Trav's eyes were soft and his voice was husky as he whispered, "Me."

Alicia's stomach swooped and she had to bite at her lip to keep from agreeing. He had no clue how badly she wanted him, how much she'd missed him over the years, but she was going to stay strong if it killed her. Trav didn't want to give up his lifestyle of fast cars and faster women. Why was he doing this to her?

"I've already traveled that route. I think I'll take a hard left instead." She spun from him and hurried to her room, locking the door and leaning against it, feeling guilty that she'd been so harsh with him, but it was the only way to keep her distance. She groaned and pounded her head against the door. How was she going to survive if he looked at her like that again?

CHAPTER FIVE

Trav had gone to the gym at five a.m. and had the place pretty much to himself. He'd been grateful for the privacy as he set up a circuit and pounded through weight sets, then did burpees until sweat covered his body. He couldn't get Alicia's words out of his mind. "I've already traveled that route. I think I'll take a hard left instead." What did that mean? He groaned and forced himself to do twenty more pull-ups. He was pretty sure it meant she didn't want him.

Then why did she look at him like she used to, like she still felt the same way as she had when they'd first met at the racetrack? They'd been married shortly after they both graduated with their undergrads then went on to law school together, though he took most of his classes online so he could continue training and racing. He'd been happier than he'd ever been in his life—racing and having success, but most of all having Ally by his side.

When her dad had been killed, she'd changed, withdrawing from him. Then she claimed he'd cheated on her, with Holly of all people, and he'd been ticked to no end. He would never cheat on her, but her accusations had been the unraveling of their marriage. The final straw was when she'd never shown up to the Daytona 500, even though he had roses, a diamond pendant, and all her favorite foods waiting in his box. Holly had promised to talk to Alicia during the race and explain that she had made an awkward pass at Trav that the media had unfortunately captured, but he had never cheated or initiated any of it. But Alicia had escaped to Wyoming, pregnant with Preston and determined to have nothing to do with Trav. She'd succeeded, too, avoiding him when he came to visit and sending her brother with Preston for visits. He was miserable without her, and she didn't seem affected by him at all.

He returned from the gym to find Alicia in the main area, dressed in a pink tank top and tight black pants. He hated how his body reacted to her beautiful shape. Her eyes traveled over him and she bit at her lip. Maybe she at least thought he was kind of attractive. Not that that would help much in the end, but his battered ego would take anything about now.

"Preston's still asleep," she said. "Are you okay if I go work out?"

"Sure. I'll order us room service."

Her lips pulled down, but she didn't respond as she hurried out of the suite, leaving her light floral scent in her wake. It was like a springtime bouquet of lilacs—sweet and succulent. Dang. He needed to go pound weights for at least another hour. He ordered a bunch of food and settled for another couple rounds of push-ups and burpees in the main area, then took a long shower. He stayed in his room and responded to emails and requests from Holly about some commercials and different events he'd need to attend before the NASCAR series started up in a few weeks.

The exterior door opened and closed, but he forced himself to not rush out into the living area and see how Alicia looked all sweaty from the gym. He squeezed his eyes shut tight and gritted his teeth.

A few minutes later he heard the doorbell and hurried to answer it before it woke Preston up. Little guy probably needed to sleep a lot more than adults did. Trav hadn't slept well at all with Alicia's rejection imprinted in his cerebral cortex.

Trav got the door and gestured their friend Drew from Jamaica in. "Hey, you get around."

Drew laughed. "I help in buffet on first day before room service orders get busy."

"Gotcha. Thank you."

"No problem, mon."

Alicia's bedroom door opened and she strode out. Her hair was wet and looked almost brown as it trailed down her back. She was wearing a simple tank top dress that highlighted her curves too well.

The young man grinned. "Happy day, my beautiful lady."

"Thank you." Alicia smiled, and Trav felt that jealousy in his gut again. What was wrong with him? The lady wanted nothing to do with him and he couldn't be defensive and jealous of every man that complimented her.

"Enjoy." Drew walked out of the suite, the door swinging shut behind him.

The silence was heavy.

"Hungry?" Trav managed.

"Starved."

"Should we wake up Preston?"

She looked like she wanted to say yes, but she shook her head. "I wanted to talk to you about something first."

Trav felt hope stir inside of him. Maybe she didn't mean what she said last night. Maybe they had a chance.

He gestured toward the table. She sat, and he rolled the cart closer and uncovered the trays of food. She served herself some eggs, yogurt, and fruit. Trav poured her a cup of apple juice from the carafe. It had always been her favorite.

"Thank you," she murmured.

Trav filled his plate with a veggie and ham omelet and a bowl of muesli filled with nuts and dried fruit. He couldn't stand the wait much longer, so before he took a bite, he got it out there. "What did you want to talk about?" He sounded like an eager boy asking Santa Claus for his dream bike.

Alicia's green eyes were wary. She knew what he was thinking. "This." She gestured to the dishes of food.

"Something's wrong with breakfast?" All his hopes died. He was dreaming of reconciliation and she was concerned about room service.

Alicia scooped up some yogurt and ate it before saying, "You're going to think I'm silly, but I've worked really hard to give Preston a normal, middle-class life. Teach him to work hard and not think he's entitled to stuff because he has a famous, wealthy dad."

Trav nodded. That was admirable, actually, but why did it feel like he was lacking because he was rich and famous?

"I don't want you spoiling Preston this week."

"Sorry. I'm going to spoil him. I don't get to see him near enough." She couldn't take the main joy in his life away from him, making Preston smile. He was going to do all in his power to "spoil" his child. Yes, that wasn't fair to her when she had to do the daily grind and keep Preston grounded, but she was the one who'd left. If she hadn't, they could deal with all of this together, every day. He forced his thoughts away from that again. She'd made it pretty clear she wasn't interested.

"Trav."

He hated and loved the way she said his name. Hated it because he didn't hear it near enough on her lips. Loved it because it made him feel ten feet tall and like he mattered, even if he never won another race.

"Preston loves you."

He nodded. He knew his boy's love was genuine and not because of the fun things they always did, his money, or his celebrity status.

"Going on this cruise is spoiling enough. I'm not saying we can't do all the fun things this ship and these islands offer, but can you please not go overboard? Spend like a normal person who's scrimped and saved to take their son on the trip of a lifetime."

"What does that even mean?" She was ticking him off now. Preston was eight. He wasn't going to analyze how much money everything cost or if he was getting special privileges. Then again, maybe kids did notice things like that, and he didn't want to ruin Preston's grateful attitude by teaching him that he was entitled to have everything handed to him.

"You don't order everything on the room service menu. We go to breakfast at the buffet like most everyone else."

"Room service costs like eight bucks."

Her cheeks colored. "Oh. Well, I guess room service is okay, but we don't need to cut to the front of lines or rent out the entire flow rider. We can wait in line like everybody else."

His forehead wrinkled. "But Preston hates lines."

"He still needs to learn to wait and not think he's something special."

"He *is* something special."

"I know that, but so is every other child out there to his or her parents. Right?"

"Okay." His rational mind knew she was right, but it didn't mean he had to like it. He was used to special privileges and didn't like waiting in lines any more than his son did. "So what do you expect of me again?"

"No private preferences. Wait in line. Book normal shore excursions that middle-class folks from Michigan would book."

His hackles rose. "Well, at least you're not throwing me right down to lower-class. What is this, the caste system?"

Laughing, she said, "It'll be fun to see you not be the top dog all the time."

But he *was* the top dog, top of his sport and wealthier than any man had a right to be. Women flung themselves at him—well, every woman but Alicia. He didn't like what she was asking of him, but he'd prove to her he could do it, and if it was what was best for Preston, he'd wade through crocodile-infested waters.

"Do you think you can handle it? You might have to take a taxi or a bus. Scary."

"I think I can handle it." Yes, he liked high-class treatment, but he wasn't afraid of not being pampered. He'd spent his fair share of time mucking out stalls, and though his parents had been wealthy they hadn't been very interested in him, so he'd learned how to take care of himself when he was pretty young. He scooted his chair closer to hers and leaned in. "Do you think *you* can handle being this close to me all week?"

Alicia's chest rose and fell in quick little pants. Trav's eyes dipped down to the smooth skin of her neck, then back to her eyes. He knew with a moment's satisfaction that she wasn't completely immune to him, no matter what she'd said last night.

Preston's door popped open and he raced to the table. "Bacon? How many strips can I have, Pops?"

"Have the whole plate if you want, bud."

"Yes!" Preston kissed his fingers and pressed them toward the heaven. "Thank you for blessing me, Lord. I love bacon! Thank you, thank you!"

Trav chuckled and the tension in the room broke. He wished Alicia would've been forced to answer, but it was probably for the best. If she'd shot him down completely again, he didn't know if he could handle it.

Alicia dressed carefully for dinner. The day had been relaxed and fun. Trav had eased up on the meaningful looks a little bit and they'd both played with their boy like little kids—rock climbing, miniature golfing, swimming, ice skating, and even waiting in line to do the stand-up surfing a few times. She was impressed with the way Trav had taken her request. She'd been afraid the wealthy, powerful man he'd morphed into over the years would scoff at her worries. Trav was a good guy, just not her good guy anymore.

She couldn't fasten her necklace because she regularly gnawed her fingernails down when she was reviewing briefs, so she carried it with her out into the living area. Preston was pretty adept at putting her jewelry on. Preston wasn't in the main area yet, but Trav was.

Her eyes traveled over him and she hoped she didn't hyperventilate. How could one man look that good? He was in a navy blue fitted suit that outlined his broad shoulders, trim waist, and muscular thighs. His smooth, deeply tanned skin was so tempting, she wanted to touch it just for old time's sake. His beard only added to his good looks. His eyes caressed her, and she couldn't help but sigh.

"Ally. You look so beautiful."

She did a little twirl in the sleeveless floral dress, knowing the skirt would float up and show off her legs. When she stopped, Trav was looking at her with a hunger in his eyes that she'd missed almost as much as his touch, and his tender words, and his kiss. Oh no, she needed to stop this train of thought right now.

"You look pretty good yourself," she managed. "I like your ... tie."

She motioned to the pale yellow tie that complemented the blue of the suit. Fingering the necklace nervously, she wondered if she should holler for Preston. Using their son as a buffer to keep Trav from drawing her in with his good looks and smooth charm was the best plan she had.

His eyes traveled over her again. "Can I help you with your necklace?"

Don't do it, girl, her mind begged, but she ignored her rational thoughts and extended the silver chain with her "favorite mother" pendant on it to him. Trav strode toward her and took the necklace, brushing her fingers in the process. He smelled so good. Who in the heck produced hot men's cologne like that? Did it really have woman-drawing pheromones in it, or was that just her excuse for having no self-control around this man?

She was frozen by the smolder in his eyes. Alicia managed to turn her back to him and lift her hair. Trav pulled the necklace around, his fingers deliberately grazing her collarbone. Her body couldn't help but react with a warmth spreading from her abdomen out. Dang him.

He took his time fastening the clasp, his fingers doing a number on her skin the entire time. Her stomach swooped and she ached to turn around and capture a moment, or his lips—either would work nicely.

His hands moved to her shoulders and her body trembled in response. When she felt his lips on her neck, she couldn't help but let out a little moan, fire rushing through her.

"Ally," he whispered, his voice deep, husky, and inspiring.

Alicia could not remember why she had to stay strong, but she instinctively pulled away and said, "Trav, please don't."

His hands dropped to his side. She couldn't look at him. Hurrying to Preston's door, she swung it open. "Do you need any help, bud?"

He glanced up, buttoning his shirt. He was in gray slacks and a striped dress shirt. They were both wrinkled, but he looked adorable. He'd even tried to comb his dark hair. "You look pretty, Momma."

"Thanks, bud."

Preston finished his buttons and walked to her, extending his arm. "Dinner, beautiful lady?"

Alicia laughed, although it came out a little shaky with the anxiety she was feeling over Trav's advances and the looming hours of this trip where she might fall prey to her ex-husband's charm at any time. She took her son's elbow and walked into the main area. Trav smiled at both of them. She hoped only she noticed how lackluster his smile was.

They went down to dinner with Preston between them. Preston. This trip was about Preston, not about her and Trav, but was their boy going to understand when the vacation was over and they weren't a family anymore?

The dining room was extravagant—three stories, chandeliers, gorgeous paintings and decorations. Their server, Chakib, greeted them warmly. Preston awkwardly pulled out Alicia's chair, then tried to push it back in. Trav chuckled and helped him. Chakib handed them menus and then Mayara brought them bread and water, giving Preston a brief hug that had him beaming.

Alicia studied her menu, but couldn't help but glance over the top of it at Trav. Unfortunately, he was studying her. She looked down quickly.

After Chakib came and took their orders, there was nothing to do but avoid Trav's penetrating gaze. Why did he have to look at her like that? Like if she would just cave to his advances, he would be the happiest man on the planet. She knew it wasn't right for them and she had to stay strong.

Preston got a little giggly and silly when Mayara placed his napkin on his lap and brought him a Sprite. The beautiful girl had told them her story last night: she'd met her husband on the ship two years ago, and now they were able to work at the same time and have time off together. She'd been so ecstatic about their opportunities to be together. It hit Alicia hard. She'd always hated when Trav had to be away from her, instead of appreciating the time they had together. Not that it mattered now.

They were finishing their appetizers of escargot for the adults and a fruit platter for Preston when Alicia leaned closer to her boy. "Everything okay?"

He grinned and winked. "I think Mayara's really cute." He must not have realized that Mayara was right behind him, holding his main course of lamb chops and mashed potatoes.

She smiled broadly, set the plate down, and gave his shoulder a squeeze. "I think you're pretty cute too."

Preston's cheeks darkened, but his grin split his face. Alicia couldn't resist glancing at Trav. His gaze was warm as he shared a conspiratorial parent look with her. The breath whooshed from Alicia's chest. Her mom and brother adored Preston, but there was no one in the world that loved a child as much as their parent, and to share a silent communication of *Our kid is the cutest boy in the world* really hit her hard. She wanted more of that connection with Trav.

Trav's gaze stayed steady, and soon they were communicating all kinds of things silently—longing, desire, hope.

"Whoa there, little man," said a voice over Preston's shoulder.

Alicia ripped her gaze from Trav's and looked over. The head waiter, Tom, was laughing as Preston had half of his pork chop jabbed on his fork and tried to chew it.

Preston quickly set the meat down and muttered, "Sorry."

"Oh my, not again." Alicia moved to intercept, but Tom was faster. He took the fork and knife and quickly cut up the pork into bite-size pieces.

Alicia was mortified that she'd done the same thing as last night—been so caught up in Trav and neglected her son. Because of his situation at school this year, Preston was ultra-sensitive and got embarrassed when he did anything he perceived to be wrong.

"Sorry," Preston said. He often repeated words, especially if he thought he was in trouble. "I'm sorry, sir, so sorry."

Trav's deep laughter rolled across the table. "Lucky guy, getting his meat cut up by the head honcho two nights in a row."

Tom grinned and handed Preston back his knife and fork. He placed his hand over his heart. "My pleasure to serve you, little man."

"Thanks," Preston exclaimed, shoving a piece of pork in.

"Thank you," Alicia reiterated. Her worry disappeared in the light of the men's good humor about the situation, and Preston seemed to be okay.

Tom winked, bowed slightly to her, and walked off.

Alicia glanced back at Trav. "Thank you," she mouthed.

His eyebrows quirked up. "For what?"

She inclined her head toward Preston. "Keeping it happy."

He nodded, but his eyes betrayed his concern. She wondered when he was going to figure out that there was more wrong with their son than just a too-strict teacher and not making the right hockey team. Was she supposed to tell him? She didn't want him to know she was failing as a mother and she didn't want to do anything that would ruin Preston's vacation. This was a time for happiness and laughter, not heavy issues.

CHAPTER SIX

Trav was still unsettled when he woke up the next morning, but at least he had a glimmer of hope. He and Alicia hadn't had a chance to talk last night, but they'd shared some good moments with Preston. Maybe if Trav tried to slow down, things would happen naturally between them. They sure had when he fell in love with her fourteen years ago, but Alicia was different now. Still as smart, beautiful, and intriguing, but she was also guarded and leery, especially of him.

It was hard to admit that he'd gotten so used to women groveling for his attention that it was a sting to his pride that the one woman he wanted was nearly impossible to get. He went for a jog around deck twelve, listening to Foreigner and enjoying the view of Labadee, Haiti, as the boat slowly pulled into port—the lush, green mountains and tan, sandy beaches with true blue waters were beautiful.

He returned to the suite and ordered room service. She'd said that was okay, right? With her plea for him to act like a middle-class person, he wasn't sure what boundaries she would take exception to. He showered, dressed in a swimsuit and T-shirt, and waited in the main area, catching up on emails, until Preston burst out of his room. "I just saw the island! Can we go ride the zip line now?"

"Sure thing." Trav grinned at his son's exuberance. Being around his boy created the absolute best moments of his life. "We just need to wait for your mom."

"I'll go wake her up." Preston tore into Alicia's room, and Trav felt a pang of jealousy. He wished he could wake Alicia up. He vividly remembered how she looked in the morning, with her golden-brown hair tousled and her green eyes sleepy. He wondered if she still slept in those silky tank tops and shorts that showed off her shoulders and legs so well, or if she was more practical now and wore flannel or something. He tried to force himself to imagine flannel.

"Good morning, sweetheart," he heard her say to Preston. His breath caught. He wanted to be the one she said "good morning, sweetheart" to. He shook his head, relieved when a sharp rap came at the door and their Jamaican buddy brought breakfast in. He didn't need to remember Alicia waking up in silky nightclothes.

Preston came back into the main area. "She's going to shower quick so we can go."

"Okay," Trav managed through a constricting throat. Now he was picturing her in the shower. He passed a hand over his face. It was brutal to still be in love with your ex-wife.

Preston said a quick prayer over the food, Trav adding his own silent plea that he could stop imagining Alicia in inappropriate situations and treat her with respect, and then they dug into the food. Alicia walked out of her room as they were finishing, dressed in a one-piece white swimsuit with a floral sarong around her waist. Trav choked on his orange juice. The white was the perfect complement to her tan and firm shoulders, and the neckline plunged enough that he was back to imagining her in the shower.

"Hey, Momma. Let's go!" Preston jumped up.

Alicia grinned at him. "Go brush your teeth and grab your flip-flops."

"You got it, lady."

Alicia's gaze transferred to Trav, and he stood slowly. Her eyes swept over him and he wondered if she liked what she saw, wondered if she ever imagined him in the shower.

"Good morning."

"Yeah, um, you hungry?" Trav rubbed at the back of his neck. He couldn't agree to the good morning. He was almost as wound up as he was before a race.

"I'm still full from last night." She pulled a face. "And I didn't wake up to exercise."

She'd always been too hard on herself. Trav had tried throughout their marriage to explain that she was perfect to him and she didn't need to push herself so hard, but she'd never believed him.

She grabbed a water bottle and took a long swallow. Trav watched in fascination. Her neck was smooth and had always been irresistible to him. When he'd put her necklace on and kissed her neck last night, he had been transported back to happier times. Then she'd stepped away and reality crushed his dreams again.

Preston tore back out of his room. "My first island! Let's do this."

Trav shook himself back to reality and hurried to his room to brush his teeth and grab his key card, money clip, sunglasses, and a hat. He wanted to make this day perfect for Preston. If only Alicia could see that giving Trav a chance would be the best thing for their son. He smiled to himself. Now that was a good idea. That angle might be the only hope he had.

A personal escort walked with them off the ship and to their own private cabana. The cabana was elevated above the beach on the bay side, and they looked out over families playing in the sand and the calm water. A waterslide wound down the mountain, and a bunch of blow-up water toys were secured in the bay. They were signed up to do the zip line at two this afternoon. It was on the opposite side of the little bay, swooping down over the ocean.

Preston settled into a cushioned chair and put his hands behind his head. "Ah, this is the life."

Alicia held back a laugh. "I give him five minutes until he's bored and ready to go," she whispered to Trav.

"I'm betting on ten," Trav said back.

She smiled, knowing she'd probably win that bet and liking that they had inside adult conversations. "I thought we were going to tone things down." She gestured to the cabana.

"Sorry," Trav said, not looking sorry at all. "My assistant set up all the shore excursions." He adopted a pious look. "If we don't do them, that would be wasting money."

Alicia couldn't argue with that, although she didn't like the thought of his "assistant" being involved in planning of the trip. She wondered if the woman was bothered by Alicia being here with Trav.

A waiter came and took their drink orders. When he left, Trav sat down in the lounge chair right next to hers with Preston on her other side and asked, "Standard bet, then?"

Alicia's stomach felt too warm and almost queasy. She should've eaten a little breakfast. "I'm sure you have your own masseuse now." She'd done massage therapy school at nights during her undergrad while she was on scholarship and used the income to put herself through law school.

"I've never had a massage as good as yours." Trav stared at her with those deep brown eyes.

Trav wasn't trained in massage, but she remembered the massages he gave very well, and with a little guidance from her, his strong hands had become very adept. They used to laugh because he'd struggled to keep his hands from wandering. She swallowed hard and tried to forget those memories.

"Let's go do the slide now." Preston sat up quickly, his relaxation at an end.

"Winner, winner." Alicia pumped her hands in the air.

"Don't you want your strawberry daiquiri first?" Trav asked Preston, winking at her.

"Oh, yeah." Preston leaned back again. "I've got to chill with a cold drink in my hand."

They both laughed, but Alicia glanced at Trav and shook her head. "That was tricky."

"This is one of your massages we're talking about."

She smiled then reclined into the comfortable lounge and closed her eyes. The waiter brought their drinks a few minutes later, and Trav beamed as he took a sip of a margarita. "Who's the winner now?"

Alicia sucked some icy goodness of piña colada down and tried to be nonchalant at the prospect of working on Trav's muscular body. The only person she was kidding was herself.

"What'd you win, Dad?" Preston asked.

"A massage from Mom."

Alicia liked the way he'd said that a little too much. It wasn't "from your mom" or "from Alicia." It was "from Mom," like they were a happy little family, but she couldn't let her mind wander that way.

"Oh, cool." Preston slurped up his drink, then set it on the small table. "Let's go now."

They hurried to keep up as he practically ran down the steps, across the beach, and up to the slide. The line for the slide was long and Preston got bored quickly. Eventually his turn came, and he sat down in the flow of water and gave them a thumbs-up. "Ciao ciao for now."

Alicia laughed and waved him off. Trav gestured for her to go next. She pushed off with her hands and then lay back on the slide. There wasn't enough water flow or height drop or something—the slide was really slow and boring. She was only halfway down when she heard, "Ally!"

Sitting up, she glanced over her shoulder just as Trav bumped into her from behind. He wrapped his arms around her waist and pulled her back against him.

"Sorry," he said, but there was laughter in his voice. "I'm a lot heavier, so I went faster."

"I couldn't get going fast at all." Yet pressing against Trav's body like this got her adrenaline spiking aplenty.

He chuckled, and she felt its familiar rumble against her back. They puttered along, the water rushing around their bodies, as they were both sitting up. "Do you want to go fast?"

"I'm kind of a slow-moving girl," she said.

"Take a chance. You might like it."

Alicia glanced over her shoulder at him. There were droplets of water on his smooth, dark skin. She could take a chance on a water-slide, just not on him. "Let's do it."

He laughed and lay back, pulling her on top of him. She could feel his chest arch and they sped off down the slide. "You go faster if you stay on shoulder blades and heels," he said against her neck.

Alicia shivered, her stomach swooping as they plunged down the slide. They whooshed out at the bottom, where Preston was waiting for them. "You guys got to go together. No fair!"

Alicia pushed out of Trav's arms and struggled to her feet. "We weren't supposed to go together, but your dad is too fast and he caught me."

"Always fun to catch you." Trav stood, and Alicia admired each muscle in his upper and lower body. He was even more defined than she remembered him.

"Oh." Preston sounded disappointed. "The slide was kind of lame. Can we try the climbing walls and slides and stuff?" He pointed toward all the blow-up toys that were secured in the bay. There were obstacle courses, giant slides, and one towering white blow-up that looked like a climbing wall with handles instead of handgrips.

"Sure."

Trav and Alicia trailed behind Preston, stopping to slip into their flip-flops and then going to the counter to get the right wristband for the blow-up toys.

"We have to wait until the next group goes out," Trav told Preston.

"I hate waiting," Preston muttered.

Trav arched an eyebrow at Alicia.

"I know," she said, "but it's good for us to learn to be patient."

"Aw, Mom. Not now."

Alicia's face flared. It wasn't fun to be the Mom nag, but he did need to learn these lessons.

"Do you want to go swim while we wait?" Trav suggested.

"Sure!" Preston ran for the water.

Trav touched her arm. "Sorry. Did I handle that wrong?"

"No." She shook her head. "It's just hard. The kid has no patience."

"He's eight."

"True." Trav was right. Most eight-year-olds weren't the epitome of patience, but it seemed like every time she turned around there was something else she needed to teach her boy.

They waded into the warm water, feeling the stickiness of the salt water and swimming and splashing until their time was called for the "aqua adventure." Strapping on life jackets, they jumped off the side of a long dock and swam for the closest platform, a green obstacle course. Alicia pulled herself out of the water and followed Preston onto the ramp, then across different obstacles. The whole thing was so slick, she slid off the side of the skinny balance beam.

She could hear Trav's throaty laughter as his hands slipped under her arms and he plucked her out of the water. He set her next to him, straddling the balance beam.

"How do you do that?" she asked.

"What?"

"Lift me like that."

"Despite the fact that I sit on my rear and push on the gas, I actually am an athlete." He winked and grinned.

"Hmm. You wouldn't know it."

He reached for her, but she laughed and scrambled on her knees off the balance beam and toward the next obstacle. Trying to run up the slick slide, she crashed back into the water before she had a chance to even grab for something stable. She got a mouthful of salt water and spit it out, blinking to clear her eyes.

She swam away quickly so Trav wouldn't lift her up again. A little distance would be helpful right now.

"Why do you keep falling, Momma?" Preston asked from the top of the obstacle that had just dumped her. "Whee!" He slid down the other side and called, "Try it, Dad."

Trav pumped his eyebrows at her. "Watch how the athlete does it."

Before Alicia could respond, he ran and leapt onto the slide, his hands clinging onto the sides. He slipped and flipped into the water, splashing her.

"Yeah, the professional athlete rocked that one." She laughed and splashed some water back at him.

Trav charged through the water like a shark. Alicia hurried to swim away, but he grabbed her around the waist and easily tossed her. She splashed into the water, feeling like a little kid.

"Do you wanna do the iceberg?" Preston was suddenly floating beside them.

Alicia felt awful that she hadn't even noticed where her son was or what obstacle he'd fallen off of. Trav needed to stop distracting her. "Sure," she agreed, though she wondered how they were going to climb up the forty-foot-tall white monstrosity.

It was the only toy that didn't have a lot of people on it. The slides looked a lot more popular and fun as people easily climbed up the side with rungs and then slid down the slick part.

They swam slowly to the iceberg and Alicia tipped her head back. It was really high. Preston tried to pull himself up. He made it up the first few rungs, and then Trav pushed him up a few more, but then he stopped about ten feet above the water. His little body was trembling and he looked like he didn't want to move. Alicia knew he didn't love heights. She was surprised he wanted to do the zip line but he'd done one in Jackson Hole and loved it.

"I don't like this. I'm going to fall back into the water."

"Okay." Trav moved out of his way.

Preston let go and made a good splash. He wiped his eyes clean. "Okay, Mom. Your turn."

Alicia wasn't sure she could make it any higher than Preston had, but she didn't want to admit that in front of Trav. She worked out every morning and she had a competitive streak. She grabbed on to the lower rungs and started to pull herself up, but almost let go of the handles when Trav put a hand on her rear and gave her a shove.

"What are you *doing?*"

"Just trying to be a gentleman, darlin'."

Alicia scrambled up several more handles and out of his grasp. "Gentlemen don't grab lady's derrieres."

Trav chuckled and she heard Preston ask, "What's a derriere?"

"You're dealing with that question." Alicia glanced down at the two of them, but almost lost her grip on the handles again. Why did the power of that smile have such an effect on her? She could handle herself in any courtroom, but get Trav anywhere in the vicinity with a grin on his handsome mug and she couldn't think straight.

Determined, she pulled herself up rung over rung. She was over the big lip and only had about ten feet more to go. Preston and Trav were cheering for her. She glanced down, and her stomach dropped. She didn't like heights much more than Preston did. How in the world was she going to get down? There was no slide, just rungs and more rungs. Could she climb back down without slipping?

Her stomach churned and her palms grew slick. She looked down to find a foothold, but missed it. Her right hand pulled from the rung and her left arm was too tired from climbing to support her. Screaming, she plunged down toward the water. Her feet hit the water, but her abdomen smacked against something solid. The oxygen whooshed out of her and she gasped in a mouthful of tepid seawater as her face dipped forward.

Trav lifted her upright and she spit the water out. He grunted. "You okay?"

"No," she managed. She drew in a ragged breath, unable to find the oxygen she needed. "What did I hit?"

"Me."

Her eyes snapped to his face. "Oh, Trav. Are you okay?"

He nodded, a mischievous look replacing the pain in his eyes. "I'm going to need that massage tonight even more than I thought."

Alicia had hoped he'd forgotten about that. Apparently not.

———

Trav didn't let on how much his lower back hurt, but Alicia had really wrenched it when she fell on him. It wasn't her fault at all; he just hadn't expected her to fall and had gotten in her way.

He made it through the rest of the blow-up toys, the zip line tour, and getting back to the ship and having dinner. Alicia kept giving him looks like she knew he was hurting, but she didn't say anything in front of Preston, who was more than happy to do sports trivia during dinner and keep them entertained.

They went to an illusionist show after dinner. The guy was truly impressive, making a snowmobile disappear and reappear behind them and creating real snow in the air, but Trav could hardly stand to sit there. He squirmed and fidgeted.

Alicia leaned close to him and he caught a whiff of her perfume—

the perfect combination of springtime flowers and sunshine. "You okay?" she whispered.

"Sure." He reached over and squeezed her hand. "Just waiting for my massage."

"Slow down, cowboy." Her face tightened and she moved her hand out from under his, but that left his hand sitting on her thigh. He smiled, not minding that at all. Alicia's entire body tightened and she murmured, "Trav."

"Hmm." He leaned in close and his lips brushed the smooth skin of her neck.

She flinched away from him. "Your hand." She inclined her head to her leg.

"Still attached to my body," he teased.

"It doesn't need to be attached to my leg," she whispered back.

"I don't see why not."

Alicia's beautiful face screwed up in the cutest expression. "Please," she whispered.

Trav sighed and removed his hand. How could he not cave to that sweet request? He focused on Preston's enraptured face instead of the magician. His son looked a lot like him, but some of his expressions were identical Alicia's. It made Trav love her even more, which wasn't smart given the fact that this vacation hadn't produced any of the attraction he'd hoped to rekindle in her for him.

Preston wanted ice cream on the way back from the show, so they stopped at the Baskin-Robbins on the promenade. Trav hated that he just wanted this evening to be over, take some ibuprofen, and go to sleep. Would Alicia really give him a massage? She freaked out every time they touched, so he didn't have a lot of hope.

They made it back to the room and Alicia offered a quick prayer, then took Preston in to sing to him. Trav downed four Ibuprofen, then lay down on his bed, trying to stretch out his back. He left his door open. Miracles might happen and she might come. He closed his eyes, not sure if he believed in miracles anymore.

Alicia listened to Preston's slow, even breaths. He'd been asleep for a few minutes, but she hadn't worked up the nerve to walk into the living area. She didn't know if she could handle massaging Trav. Even though she'd done it professionally, it was just different when she touched Trav. She wasn't ready for that level of connection with him again. She might never be.

Slowly, she stood and eased out of Preston's room, closing the door behind her. Her eyes darted around the main room. No sign of Trav. She started toward her bedroom, but paused at his open door. When she fell off the iceberg, she'd hurt him. He was an athlete who needed to be at the top of his game when his season started next month.

If she stayed professional and detached, she could help him feel better. She owed him that for hurting him, even though it was unintentional. Anticipation raced through her. She was going to get to touch Trav again. No, wait. She was, but she was going to be calm and rational about it.

Steeling her spine, she marched into his room. He was lying on his bed with his eyes closed. She should've been relieved to not have to massage him, but she'd let herself get excited about it.

Alicia's gaze traveled over his face and body, outlined by the light from a lamp. He was so fit and ... manly. That smooth, tanned skin of his face was irresistible. His short facial hair made him even more appealing. Creeping closer, she gently touched his cheek with her palm. The hair was soft just like she remembered.

She saw his lips turn up an instant before he grasped her wrist and tugged her on top of him.

"Trav!" she cried out in surprise.

Trav secured his arms around her lower back and held her against his chest. "Need somethin', darlin'?"

Alicia lay perfectly still, feeling his heart beating against her own chest. Memories and desire crashed through her. She'd always loved being in his arms. Her body stiffened. And so had a lot of other women, apparently.

"I thought you were injured." She struggled to free herself.

"I am." Trav released her with a groan.

Alicia stood, brushing her skirt back down into place. The nerve of him, pulling her onto the bed with him. What if she had told him yes, she needed something, she needed him? The thoughts that hurtled through her brain terrified her. She didn't need him. She was doing just fine on her own, thank you very much. "Would you like some help with your back?" she asked stiffly.

"If you could. I really did a number on my lower back."

"You did or I did?"

Trav smiled. "I was the one in the wrong spot at the wrong time." His smile faded and he stood, gazing down at her much too seriously. "Story of my life."

"What do you mean?" she whispered, captivated by his deep brown eyes.

"Missing your dad's funeral, all the stuff in the tabloids with other women."

Alicia's breath caught. Oh no. He wasn't doing this to her. She'd jump overboard before she hashed all of this out with Trav. Their relationship was dead because of much bigger reasons than he'd listed—over and done. "Don't, Trav. Please."

He traced his thumb down her cheek. "Are you ever going to be ready to talk to me?"

Alicia bit at her lip. "This was a big step, coming on the cruise. Can we please just take it slow?" She was such a liar. She had no intentions of ever having the deep talk he wanted to have. At this moment deflection was the best tool she had.

His eyes were full of uncertainty and conflict, but he nodded. "Anything you want, Ally."

"Let's look at your back."

Trav crossed his arms and tugged his shirt up and over his head. Alicia's mouth went dry and her pulse pounded in her throat. She stared at the nicely formed muscles of his chest for several seconds before forcing her gaze up to his face. He was grinning cockily at her.

"You like that?" he asked in a deep, husky voice.

Be professional, be professional.

"Please lie face down on the bed," she instructed.

Trav's smile grew infuriatingly wide, but he complied. Alicia's hands trembled. Here was this perfect specimen lying there in just a pair of shorts, and she was supposed to touch him and stay detached? He turned his face toward her. "You okay?"

"Yeah, um. I don't have any oil. I'll just see if I have any lotion that doesn't smell like a girl."

"I don't mind smelling like you."

Alicia hurried from the room and into her bathroom. She rummaged through her products, but only found her wild honeysuckle body lotion. Well, he'd said he didn't mind.

She slowly returned to Trav's room. He'd rolled over onto his back again and had his hands clasped behind his head. Every muscle from his biceps down to his abdomen was on perfect display. Did they have a pinup calendar for NASCAR drivers, and was he Mr. January?

His eyes opened as she approached the bed again. They were laser-focused on her, and Alicia knew she wasn't going to be able to keep her distance if he kept looking at her like that. "Roll over, please," she said.

"Okay." He lay face down on the king bed and tilted his head so he was looking at her. "Thanks for helping me."

"Sure."

"Is it going to be a pain without a massage bed?"

"A little."

"You can climb up onto the bed next to me if it makes it easier."

Alicia's face went hot just imagining climbing up next to him on that bed. "Okay, rule number one during a massage—no talking."

"Why?"

"I'm not going to be able to get in touch with your body if you distract me with nonstop diatribe."

"I'll let you get in touch with my body anytime, darlin'."

"Shush!" She opened her fingers and thumb, then clamped them tight together. "That was the symbol. If I give you the shush symbol, you need to shush." She was hot and cold all over. They were only on night three and she wasn't going to survive if he kept talking like that.

Trav chuckled and closed his eyes. Luckily, he didn't open his mouth again either.

Alicia rubbed some lotion between her palms and reached for his back, but he was right that it would be awkward without a massage table. Left with no choice, she crawled onto the bed so she could reach him properly.

Trav opened his eyes and grinned. "Good idea, eh?"

She made the shushing symbol with both hands, and he laughed. Alicia couldn't help but laugh with him. Placing her hands on his back, she paused to ground herself. His body had always been her weakness, and not just because it was so fabulous. There was no way to resist the connection between them when she touched him.

She started slowly, working on the muscles of his lower back and warming them up. He groaned at one point and she felt bad hurting him, but she couldn't help him without getting deep into the muscle tissue. She could feel the knot where his back muscles had tightened in response to the acute injury of her falling on him.

"Where did I hit you?" she asked.

"I tried to dodge to the right, but I couldn't move very fast in the water, so you tagged me on the left side of my abdomen."

"You'll need to roll over again."

He rolled quickly and grabbed on to her waist. Alicia gasped and scrambled back a few inches. Trav didn't say anything, just lay there looking up at her with a smoldering gaze. Finally, his hands dropped and she was able to ignore him and work the muscles of his abdomen. My, oh, my, he was fit.

"Do you have a personal trainer?" It was a dumb question no matter how she looked at it.

He grinned. "Yeah. His name's Greg and he thinks it's hilarious to push me until I whimper."

She met his gaze. "I've never see you whimper." Wrong thing to say, again.

"Really? You make me whimper all the time." He winked.

She finished working the injury, ignoring his gaze, then climbed to the end of the bed and checked his leg length. He'd always had a slightly longer right leg, and as she tugged on them, she could see it was still the same. That was good news. "Okay, roll over again."

He complied slowly. Moving back next to him, she worked through the muscles of his mid and upper back and his neck. His shoulders were really tense.

"Have you been under a lot of stress?" she asked as she worked his right trapezoid.

"You mean since coming on the cruise?"

"Vacation shouldn't cause you stress."

"Vacation doesn't. You do, darlin'."

She'd always loved when he called her that. Some men saying it might be demeaning or outdated, but not Trav. But wait, why was she causing him stress? "Why me?"

Trav rolled onto his side and reached out to her, wrapping his arms around her waist. "Life's never been as good without you, Ally. I hoped this week might be our chance to reconnect."

Alicia stared at him. His eyes were sincere and filled with raw hope. She'd been able to stay sort of professional throughout the massage and she was proud of that, but now, as she knelt close to him and his hands tugged her closer, she knew escape was the only way to keep from falling under his charm.

She fully intended to push away from him, but her hands had better ideas. They'd been trained to appreciate muscle, and his chest was inspiring. She trailed her fingers over his chest, her stomach smoldering.

Trav's eyes were intent on her face. He rolled back onto his back and tugged her down on top of him. Oh, no. She could not stay strong in this position, and giving in to Trav would only cause them and their son heartache.

"No," she murmured.

"No?" Trav's voice was full of confusion.

Alicia shook her head and pulled from his grip. She sprung off the bed and only stopped when she was safely in the doorway. "I hope your back is okay," she managed.

Trav sat up and blinked at her. He reached out a hand. "Ally."

Alicia felt like her body was frozen, but if she tried to move she would run back to Trav. "Don't do it," she muttered to herself. Finally, she dredged up the strength to ignore the plea in his eyes and the need to touch his smooth skin again, and ran for her bedroom.

CHAPTER SEVEN

Trav got back from the gym a little later than he had the past few mornings because of the simple fact that Alicia had him more stirred up than ever, and he hadn't slept well so he had a hard time pulling himself out of bed. His back was feeling better today, thanks to her ministrations. It was all he could do to not close his eyes and moan as he thought about her hands on him.

He inserted his key card then swung open the suite door, where Alicia was waiting. She didn't even look at him as he held the door for her and she brushed past. "Thanks. I'll be back in an hour."

"Okay," he muttered.

He'd run on the treadmill today, which luckily only hurt his back for the first few minutes; then he'd gotten warm and numb at the same time and had a decent run. He'd also been coated with sweat due to the poor ventilation in the cardio room and the heat and humidity as they traveled farther south. Did he stink? Was that why she'd rushed past him so quickly? He wished that were the reason, and not simply that she didn't want to be near him.

He checked on Preston, who was sleeping splayed out on his back with no covers on. Trav smiled, pulled the sheet and blanket up to his son's waist, and gently closed the door. He stretched for a long time, then showered and ordered a bunch of room service. Alicia would be ticked at him no matter what he did, so he was tempted to give up trying to please her. When his thoughts turned to Preston, though, he honestly wanted to cry. Didn't his son deserve an intact family? All the money in the world, and he couldn't give his son the one thing he knew he wanted, and needed, more than any other.

What if Alicia married someone else and Preston had a jerk for a stepdad? He walked out onto the main patio, staring at the open ocean, small waves sparkling in the sunshine. His gut churned at the thought of Alicia remarrying. It was some kind of miracle that she hadn't already. She was gorgeous, smart, successful, and fun. Well, fun when she wasn't mad at him.

A rap came at the door, and Trav hurried to open it.

"Hey, mon." Drew held out his hand for a fist bump and wheeled in the food and drinks.

Trav looked at the clock and realized Alicia had been gone for over an hour and a half. Was something wrong? He glanced toward Preston's door, then back to Drew. He wanted to go check on her quick, but he couldn't leave Preston alone.

Drew had finished unloading everything. "Enjoy." He headed for the door.

"Hey, can I ask you a favor?"

"Sure, mon, anything." He turned back with a smile.

"I have to run find my … wife quick, but I don't want to leave my little guy alone. He's sleeping." He inclined his chin to the closed door.

"Ah. I don't know, mon. I have deliveries to make."

Trav whipped out his wallet, pulled out a hundred-dollar bill, and shoved it at the guy. "I'll be fast. She's just across the ship at the gym."

Drew's eyes darted back and forth from the money to the door.

"I'll also call room service and tell them you were helping us out so your delivery took a little longer, and I'll leave you a really good review and extra tip at the end." Trav didn't know why he felt such an urgency to find Alicia, but he just felt like something wasn't right for her to be gone this long.

Drew rubbed his bald head for a second, then grabbed the money. "Okay. I've got a wife. I get you, mon."

That stopped Trav. "Where's your wife?"

"At home. In Ocho Rios."

"You have to leave her to work?"

"Ship is the best money I can make, mon. If I work hard, I can retire in ten years and be with my lady all the time."

Trav's stomach sank. He and Alicia were separated, but Drew was away from his wife through no fault of his own. "How soon until you see her again?"

"Two month, ten day." Drew smiled, but Trav could see he was hurting.

"Ah, I'm sorry, man."

Drew accepted that with a nod and gestured him toward the door. "Go get your girl so I can get back to work."

"Thank you. I'll be right back." Trav rushed out of the door and down the hallway. He turned the corner toward the exterior entrance and almost bumped into Alicia and some huge blond dude.

"I already told you," Alicia was saying, "I am not interested."

The guy had a hold of her arm, and fire burned inside of Trav. All rational thought left as he crossed the corridor and slammed his fist into the guy's jaw. The blond spun away from Alicia, his hands flying to his face as he squealed in pain.

"Trav!" Alicia cried out.

"You want more?" Trav asked.

The guy held up his hands and backed up a step. "Who are you?"

"I'm her husband. Don't mess with her again. Got it?"

"Yeah, but you're somebody famous." His eyes widened and he cursed softly. "You're Travis Poulsen. You're number eighty-eight. I just got hit by Travis Poulsen!"

"Go brag to your friends about it." The guy sounded like Trav had handed him a million bucks. Probably exactly what he was thinking: he could sue Trav for a million bucks. Trav didn't care. He would hit him again if he saw him touching Alicia and heard that slight tremor in her voice.

"I will! You're my favorite driver." He beamed. "Sorry about, you know, hitting on your wife. Good job, by the way, she's really hot."

Trav couldn't believe this guy.

He shoved out his hand. "No hard feelings?"

Trav forced himself to shake the crazy man's hand, though he wanted to hit him again for calling Alicia hot like she was some piece of meat.

"Sorry, ma'am." The guy nodded to Alicia, turned, and strode out the exterior door, muttering, "Travis Poulsen."

Trav turned to Alicia. "You okay?" he asked.

She just stared at him. "What are you doing?"

"Well, I thought I was protecting you."

She shook her head. "I deal with crap like that all the time. I'm fine." Her eyes widened. "Where's Preston?" She whirled and ran for their room.

Trav hurried after her. What did she mean, she dealt with crap like that all the time? Were men always hitting on her? What if she was in some deserted alley or something, what then? Had someone hurt her? Holy crap, he needed to be with her and protect her.

She made it to the door first and inserted her key card, flinging it open. "Preston!"

"Shh, mum, I think he's still asleep," Drew said. He stood from the couch and offered Trav another fist bump on the way out. "Thanks for being quick."

"No problem," Trav managed, his head still full of images of that blond guy in the hall hurting Alicia. "Thank you."

The door shut behind Drew. Alicia ran into Preston's room and was back out in seconds. She clicked the door closed and stormed up to Trav. "How dare you leave our son alone?"

Trav's brow wrinkled. "I didn't leave him alone. I left him with Drew."

"You don't know Drew from a drug smuggler. He could've hurt him."

Trav blinked. "But he's a chill guy. He wouldn't hurt him."

"You don't know that." She folded her arms across her chest, but Trav could still see that she was trembling.

"He's an employee of the ship. He wouldn't dare do anything amiss and lose his job. He told me about his wife, how he's working for ten years so he can be with her full-time."

Alicia took a deep breath and then shook her head. "When Preston comes and stays with you, do you leave him alone?"

"No!" Trav rubbed at his suddenly hot neck, not appreciating her attack at all. He was a good father. "I have a gym in my house so I work out at home, and I take Preston everywhere with me when he comes to visit. If he comes to a race, Carson or Holly are with him."

She flinched at the mention of Holly. Trav pushed a hand through his hair. Why couldn't she believe that he had no romantic interest in Holly, despite what the tabloids printed? He'd actually tried to fire Holly after the messed-up tabloid exposure that had driven Alicia away, but she'd been the sole provider for her little sister and he hadn't been able to follow through with it.

Alicia blinked, and a tear rolled past her dark lashes.

"Hey." Trav crossed the distance to her and pulled her into his arms. "I'm sorry. I got worried about you."

She sniffled and laid her head against his shoulder.

Trav closed his eyes and savored having her in his arms. She was sweaty from the gym, but he didn't care. "You okay?"

"No." She pushed out a long breath. "That guy scared me, and then I was worried about Preston."

He knew that guy had upset her more than she wanted to let on. "You really have idiots like that after you all the time?"

Alicia straightened and pushed from his arms. "I can take care of myself, Travis." She hurried into her room and shut the door.

Trav sank into a chair next to the table. He was hungry, but had little desire to eat. Alicia needed him, but she might never admit it.

They didn't get into port in San Juan until one-thirty, and then it took almost half an hour just to get off the ship because everyone was ready to go and the lines were long. Preston snuggled against Alicia, asking every few minutes why they weren't moving. Trav tried to joke with him and play the sticks game to entertain him. Alicia appreciated not having to deal with Preston by herself when he got impatient like this.

They finally made it off the ship and got directions to walk to the fort. Preston ran at first because he was so excited, but it was hot and within minutes he was tired and dragging. Trav swooped him up and put him on his shoulders. Alicia couldn't resist snapping some pictures of the two of them.

"What are you taking pictures of?" Trav asked.

"The scenery."

He smiled at her, and her breath caught. Scenery indeed. Her two boys were the best scenery she'd ever seen. *Her two boys.* She couldn't think like that. Trav wasn't hers.

They made it to the thirty-foot-thick wall that surrounded Old San Juan. It was impressive, and even more so when they got to the main fort. They explored each section, staircase, gunwale, and guardhouse. Preston loved it and Alicia took a ton of pictures.

As they emerged from the fort, they were hot and tired. A street vendor was selling hand-shaved flavored ice. Trav bought them each one. Alicia savored the piña colada–flavored ice. She hadn't realized how thirsty she was.

"Where to next?" Trav asked.

"Boogie boarding!" Preston called out excitedly. "Momma says this is the only stop where we'll have good waves."

"Good call." He winked at her, then turned and conversed with the vendor, who didn't speak much English. Trav spoke a little Spanish. All she could understand was Uber and Condado Beach.

"Gracias." Trav pulled out his phone and opened the Uber app.

"Famous race car driver uses Uber?" Alicia couldn't help but tease.

"Sometimes even us famous people don't have a limo waiting for them." Trav grinned.

"It's a hard-knock life." She laughed, but then she noticed the time on his phone. "Trav? Is that the right time?"

"Yeah, it's five, but we don't have to be at the boat until nine-thirty."

She glanced over at Preston as he slurped up his mango ice. "Yeah, but it might be too late in the day to rent boogie boards. Sunset is at six-twenty-one." She'd checked her phone about both things back on the ship. She had coverage here because it was a U.S. territory. The rentals only went until five or so on the beaches and sunset was pretty early this time of year.

"Oh." His brow wrinkled. "Let me Google shops to buy boards, then."

She nodded her thanks and finished her treat. The Uber driver came a few minutes later. He was a lanky young man, driving a Toyota 4-Runner, and could speak passable English. He thought he might be able to find them a shop and a beach that weren't too far away.

Alicia watched anxiously as the sun dipped lower and the traffic didn't move. She kept sneaking glances at Preston. He bounced in his seat. "Will we boogie board soon?" he asked.

"Sorry, so sorry. Busy time for traffic," the driver said.

"It's all right. We understand. We lost track of time." Trav glanced at Preston.

"Do you want to look at the pictures from the fort?" Alicia pulled out her phone, opened the photos app, and handed it to Preston.

"Yes, please." Preston took the device greedily. Alicia tried to monitor his device time, but it felt like a losing battle since she wasn't always around, and her mom was too tired lately to enforce rules.

Alicia leaned around the front seat and pressed her mouth close to Trav's ear. "The sun's going to go down before we find a shop or the beach," she whispered.

He turned slightly, and she could smell the sweetness of piña colada on his breath. "What do we do?" he asked back.

"Just go back to the ship and deal with it if he freaks out."

Trav nodded. His eyes locked on hers, and she had to pull back to break the connection.

"Can you take us back to the ship?" Trav asked the driver.

"Cruise ship?" the driver clarified.

"Yes, thank you."

"Sí."

The driver turned down the next street. Alicia watched Preston, dreading the moment he realized they weren't going to make it to the beach.

Ten minutes later, the driver let them out next to the pier. Preston handed over her phone and looked around in confusion at the large cruise ships and the busy port with street vendors clamoring for attention. "I thought we were going to the beach."

Alicia gnawed at her lip. "I'm sorry. We had too much fun at the fort and we ran out of time."

Preston glanced back and forth at the two of them, then went over to a low wall next to the water and sat down on it. Alicia and Trav exchanged a look before each taking a seat on either side of him.

Half a minute stretched by and Alicia waited, hoping Preston was okay and wondering what her son might reveal to Trav in the next few minutes. She hadn't told anyone but her mom and brother about his obsessive-compulsive disorder diagnosis. She wasn't sure she believed it fully herself. Yes, he was a bit quirky, but he was a good, obedient boy and he had a lot to deal with.

"You okay, bud?" Trav finally asked.

Preston glanced up at his dad. "I thought family vacation was going to be more fun than this. I thought I would have the best time of my life."

Trav reared back. "You aren't having fun?"

"Sorry, Dad. I'm sorry."

"It's okay, bud. I'd rather you be honest with me." Trav glanced at Alicia and the look in his eyes bugged her, like he was wondering if she was mean to their son or something. Preston repeated things a lot, usually sorry, goodbye, or I love you. It wasn't that big of a deal.

"I am having fun." Preston shrugged. "But not every minute. My friends all have fun every minute when they go on vacation."

Alicia wrapped her arm around him. "They might, bud, but probably not. They only tell you the best parts, and you'll do the same when you get home—you'll only remember the best parts."

Preston nodded, and she continued, "Even vacation can't be fun every minute. Sometimes you have to wait in line, or in a taxi cab. Sometimes the thing you wanted to do doesn't work out." As evidenced by today. Why hadn't she insisted they go to the beach first?

He looked at his dad, not her. "But I thought Dad would make everything good every minute."

Trav gave a forced smile. "I want to for you, bud, but your mom is right ... life isn't like that. Even vacation has some times where you might be bored or frustrated. The trick is learning to look for the positive even during those times."

Alicia nodded, hoping Preston would get the message. He sighed and stood. "Can we play shuffleboard and watch a movie together after dinner, like a family?"

Trav glanced at her.

"Sure, that'd be fun," Alicia said.

They walked slowly back to the cruise ship, went to their suite, and got changed for dinner. For some reason, Alicia found herself getting more and more frustrated. Preston didn't have some perfect life—his grandma and uncle were basically raising him, his dad lived across the country, he hated school right now, he was embarrassed that he had to meet with a therapist, he hadn't made the hockey team he wanted ... she could go on and on. She'd wanted this vacation to be perfect for him too, and already it wasn't. She blinked back tears of frustration and steeled her spine. She'd just have to try harder.

She entered the main room of the suite to find Trav in there alone. She debated going back into her room and re-entering when Preston was there to be a buffer between them. Even though today hadn't worked out right, she appreciated Trav being with them and found herself realizing more and more what it would be like to be a family.

He smiled at her, and she was caught. "You doing okay?"

Alicia shrugged and found she couldn't just pretend with him. "I feel bad. I wanted to boogie board with him in the ocean as much as he wanted to do it."

"I know." Trav hit his fist against his leg. "I hate not having everything be perfect for him."

Alicia couldn't form the words as her throat was clogging up, but she nodded her agreement.

Trav took a couple of steps closer to her. "We can boogie board together later."

"No, we can't. I researched it. This is the only stop on this cruise that has waves." She was fighting back tears. It was silly. She could take another vacation with Preston to California and go boogie boarding. Why was she buying into Preston's theories that this was their "family vacation" that had to be fun every minute and if they didn't do everything together, it would never be the same again? She knew better than Preston that this was a one-and-done family trip and they would never be all together again, but why was that making her so sad?

"Okay." Trav's voice was soothing like it had been with Preston today outside the ship when he'd been upset. "We can go boogie boarding together somewhere else. I've heard Kauai has some great boogie boarding spots." He winked, and his smile was far too intriguing to her.

"We're not going on another vacation, Trav. Stop teasing me." *Kauai.* They'd gone there on their honeymoon, but they hadn't done nearly as many touristy things as they'd planned on. A week turned out to fly by really quick. She blushed just thinking about it.

"Would you want to ... go on another vacation together?" He looked like he was holding his breath as he waited for her answer.

Alicia was being drawn in by those dark brown eyes, and they were more irresistible than Godiva chocolate. Kauai. Oh, goodness, he wasn't playing fair. She couldn't get images of that beach house in Kauai out of her head now, and goosebumps were popping up on her arms.

She shook her head to clear it and studied Preston's door. "Let's just focus on today, okay?"

Trav crossed the room in sure strides. Her gaze flew back to his. He cupped her cheek in his palm, bent close, and in a husky whisper said, "You remember Kauai, don't you?"

"Trav, please." She couldn't catch her breath. His warm, manly scent surrounded her. If he stayed this close, she was going to reach up and kiss him and show him exactly what she remembered about Kauai.

"Please what?" He leaned close enough their breath was intermingling.

"I can't. This isn't fair."

"Fair?" His eyes swept over her face, down across her lips, then back up to meet hers. "What you do to me isn't fair, Ally."

Alicia gulped. Her stomach was full of butterflies and she was feeling decidedly weak. Trav seemed to understand as he wrapped his other hand around her back and drew her body flush to his. Sadly, this didn't help the weakness in her legs, but made it more pronounced.

She leaned into him and couldn't resist wrapping her hands around his broad shoulders. She made the mistake of inhaling, and it was so familiar. It was more than his cologne it was Essence of Trav. Oh, she'd always loved his smell.

"Ally," Trav whispered then let out a soft groan that completely undid her. Before Alicia could stop herself, she covered those few inches and pressed her lips to his. Trav drew in a sharp breath, then returned the kiss with a fervor that made her lightheaded. Their lips worked in sync as if they hadn't experienced an eight-year hiatus, but kissing him was even more exciting and fulfilling than she'd remembered.

Trav framed her face with his hands and her hands trailed from his strong back through his hair, then down across the stubble of his face. She wanted to explore every part of him, a thought that made her knees go even weaker, and she grabbed on to his biceps and held on. She never wanted to let go of his strength as she gave in to the desire she'd always had for him.

Preston's door flung open. Alicia jumped backward, dislodging herself from Trav's arms and banging her back on a side table.

"Dad! What're you guys doing?"

Alicia bit at her lip. Trav looked so devastatingly handsome. She'd messed up his hair and rumpled his shirt. When had she even touched his hair? Everything was swirling in the memory of pleasure and the desire to order room service, put Preston to bed early, and pick up where they'd left off.

No! She could *not* do this again.

"I was teaching your mom something," Trav said, shooting a cocky grin her direction.

"What?" Alicia and Preston both asked at the same time.

"How much better life is when you work together." Trav winked.

Alicia was never going to be able to stay strong around him. Her mother had been cursed to love a race car driver. It must be in their genetic makeup to be dumb enough to love someone who could never fully love you back.

Alicia focused on Preston. He looked so cute in his button-down floral shirt and black shorts. She had to think about Preston, not herself. About the life Preston needed, not having both of their hearts broken when Trav went back to his own life or—as she'd always feared —got killed in a race car like her daddy had.

"Thought you weren't supposed to have to learn stuff on vacation," Preston said.

"Life's all about learning stuff, son."

"We're late for dinner." Alicia reached for the door. She'd learned plenty of life lessons from Trav. Right now being strong was more important than working together.

Trav's thoughts were a jumble throughout dinner. Alicia had kissed him, really kissed him. Yes, he had been the one to pull her close and give her the opportunity, but she had definitely crossed those last few centimeters and she had been as invested in the kiss as he had been.

He was flying high during dinner, joking with Preston, Chakib, and Mayara. Mayara's husband had a break from work and came to meet all of them. Preston got a little jealous when Mayara's husband gave her a kiss goodbye, and Trav and Alicia had exchanged an amused glance. It was a great dinner. Alicia was a little more reserved than he'd hoped she'd be after a kiss like that, but her mind was probably going a mile a minute too.

He could hardly wait to get her alone again, kiss her until she remembered Kauai, and talk about all the garbage they needed to put behind them. There was hope for him, Alicia, and Preston, and it was absolutely beautiful. He couldn't quit smiling at Preston. His little man's plan to help them become a family again was working.

After dinner, they played shuffleboard, but the wind was vicious on the decks tonight, so it sent them inside and Preston was happy to choose a movie and get settled in to watch *Robots* between both of his parents.

Trav was almost apprehensive about what might happen after the movie. He could hardly focus, but it was a contented feeling to be sitting on the couch with his little family watching a movie.

He stretched his arm behind Preston and placed it on Alicia's firm shoulder. She tensed under his fingertips. He cast a concerned glance over Preston's head, but she wouldn't turn and look at him. His mind scrambled for any reason why she wouldn't welcome his touch. She'd been quiet during dinner. Was she not as thrilled with the kiss as he'd been?

He removed his hand and wrapped it around Preston's shoulder instead. He didn't want to push her too hard, but things had to be going the right direction for them, didn't they?

Preston cuddled into him, and halfway through the movie he was snoring.

Trav gently bumped Alicia's shoulder. She jumped, and he couldn't help but scowl. What was going on with her?

"Little man's tuckered out," he said.

She smiled down at their son. "He's so cute."

"Yes, he is." Trav swooped Preston into his arms and stood. "I'll be right back," he said it in a meaningful way that he hoped she couldn't misunderstand. He was coming back to continue what they started before dinner and he wasn't going to let her slip away this time.

Alicia didn't respond, but simply stared at him. Trav walked into Preston's room, balanced the boy and pulled the covers back, then laid him down. He'd just have to sleep in his clothes tonight. He covered Preston up, then placed a kiss on his forehead. What a kid. He felt so blessed that Preston was his son.

He straightened, and anticipation of what awaited him rushed through him again. Alicia. She'd always been his dream woman, and now he was being given another shot at her. He truly was the luckiest guy he knew.

Striding from Preston's room, he shut the door softly, then turned toward the couch. It was empty. His gaze darted around the main area, but there was no golden-haired beauty waiting for him.

Her door was open. Maybe he shouldn't, but an open door was an invitation. He strode into her room. "Ally?"

No response. He turned on a light, and a quick glance was all he needed to know that the room was empty. His gut tightened. Could she possibly be waiting in his room? Ally and he both honored the sanctity of marriage and he wouldn't do more than kiss her until they exchanged vows again, but he still thought her being in his room was a sign from above. If she was ready to place that much trust in him, she was definitely ready to be a family again. Didn't people get married on cruise ships all the time? He could arrange it tomorrow if she would agree.

Trav couldn't contain his grin as he hurried from Ally's room and into his own. The lights were on, but every hope and dream withered quickly. She wasn't there. He checked the long balcony quickly just to make sure, then returned to her room and rapped on the bathroom door. Nothing. No sounds. No Ally.

Trav returned to the main room and sat on the couch, burying his head in his hands. She'd ditched him. It all came rushing back to him. The night of the Daytona 500. Ally's dad had died a few weeks before and she'd begged Trav not to race, but it was his career and he couldn't turn his back on it. He just assumed that she'd support him. Her mom had always supported her dad.

But she hadn't come to the race. Holly had told him afterward that Ally had never come. When he got home that night, she was gone. He'd been mad and acted immature and cocky and hadn't gone to her until Preston was born a few weeks later, but then he'd been turned away, her mom explaining in no uncertain terms that Ally could never love a race car driver.

Eight long years later, she still hadn't had a decent conversation with him about why she'd ditched him at Daytona or why they could never work. He'd finally forced himself to go over the divorce papers she'd already sent him, too depressed to do more than sign. He loved her so much, and if that was what she wanted, he didn't know how to fight her.

And here he was again. His hopes dashed, ditched by the woman he loved. She knew he was bound to this room with Preston asleep and he wouldn't dare leave him, especially after she'd reamed him about leaving him this morning.

Trav blew out a long breath. The message was loud and clear. Ally didn't want him, and he shouldn't have built up the dreams again in his head. Why did it have to hurt worse than slamming into the wall at Talledega?

Alicia walked the twelfth-floor outdoor track for over an hour. The wind whipped at her hair and clothes, lifting her tears and taking them away before she had to admit to how fast they were falling from her eyes. Ah, Trav. Why did he have to be so great? He smelled heavenly and he kissed even better. He'd been so cute and happy tonight, like that guy she'd fallen in love with years ago, but it had hit her as soon as their lips had separated—nothing had changed. Trav was still going to risk his life on a racetrack and she still wasn't willing to be a race widow. Even if he never died in a car, his career was more important than his family, and being alone with that knowledge hanging over her head was like being a widow anyway.

For some reason, Duke's face kept coming to her mind. He thought they were dating seriously and hadn't been happy about her going on this trip. She liked the guy, a lot. He was safe and kind and would be a great stepdad for Preston. True, his kiss did nothing for her compared to the zingers Trav could issue, but life wasn't all about sparks and electricity. Life was about reliability and comfort and ... the tears fell more quickly. Why did she have to love Trav so much?

When her feet ached from walking in flip-flops, she went down to the promenade and got herself a piece of pizza and made a cup of dark hot chocolate with two packets and extra cream. She sat by herself and savored the treat, but guilt was heavy in her belly, making it hard to even eat. Duke thought she was committed to him, and she probably should be. Trav was every bit as wonderful as she'd remembered, but she couldn't love a race car driver now any more than she could have eight years ago.

She finally threw most of her food in the garbage and climbed the six flights, easing herself into their suite. Trav was asleep on the couch, sprawled out in all his beautiful glory. She knew most women thought he was handsome, but she couldn't imagine anyone else was as drawn to him as she was.

She let herself imagine for a second that she walked boldly to the couch, lay down next to him, and whispered in his ear how much she loved him. He'd take her in his arms and ... She shook her head and tiptoed past him into her room, quietly shutting the door. She lay down on her bed without taking off her makeup or brushing her teeth. Tears came again, and she realized she didn't need to remove her makeup when she was crying it all off anyway. Dang Trav all to heck for making her want him so much when it was never going to happen for them again.

CHAPTER EIGHT

W hen Alicia woke the next morning, the sun was streaming through the edge of the curtain. She pulled it back and walked out onto the balcony. They were already docked in St. Maarten. It looked to have some decent beaches across the harbor, but the mountains weren't lush like Kauai—lots of trees, but not as green and tropical-looking.

She sighed. Why was she comparing things to Kauai now? She had to get those memories out of her mind or she'd cave to Trav faster than he shifted gears in his car.

She wandered back into her room and got ready quick, then walked into the main area. Trav was at the table, eating. There were at least a dozen trays from room service. When his gaze settled on her, she couldn't tell if he was angry about last night or just really disappointed. Either way, she was not getting into it. She gestured to the spread. "I thought we talked about pretending to be middle-class." She tried to say it jokingly, but his eyes narrowed all the same.

"I'm trying to do everything you want, but it's not really bringing any results."

It was her turn to bristle. Luckily, Preston burst out of his room right then. "You ready to go, Mom? Dad says we're going to the beach."

"Fun." She gave him a tight squeeze and he returned it. Oh, she loved her boy. She'd hold him all day if he'd let her. She glanced over his shoulder to see Trav watching them. His face had softened and he gave her a smile, then looked away.

"Do you want something to eat?" Trav asked.

Why did he have to be so good to her? He was right. He always tried to do everything she wanted and even anticipate what she might want in the future. She grabbed a container of yogurt. "Thank you."

They strolled onto the dock a few minutes later. Since the ship had been berthed for a while, there weren't any lines getting off today. At the end of the dock there was a shopping area. Local men with monkeys on their shoulders approached them. One slung an arm around Alicia and another arm around Preston and told Trav to take a picture. Trav snapped a few. Of course the guy wanted ten bucks for his trouble.

They found a taxi driver quickly who spoke pretty good English. He drove them through the town. He was an absolutely horrid driver—punching the gas, then slamming on the brake. The drive to the French side of the island stretched on and on. The driver swerved, sped up, slowed down. He was really horrible. Trav must be going nuts in the front seat. Alicia held in a giggle. The professional driver sitting in the passenger seat next to the worst driver she'd ever ridden with.

"More water, Mom," Preston said.

"Sure." She handed him a water bottle, and he chugged half of it. "Whoa. You feeling okay?"

"No." He looked a little pale. "Gonna throw up."

"Stop the car!" Alicia called out to the driver. Trav spun around just as Preston heaved all over the floor.

The driver cursed and pulled over. Alicia jumped out of the back seat and ran around, helping Preston out. He was all done at that point, so she hurried to give him a drink and attempted to wash him off. Trav grabbed one of their beach towels and swept the mess off the seat and onto the floor mat, then carefully dumped it all on the road. Alicia was impressed with how good of a job he did, even using a water bottle to clean off the floor mat and then drying the seat and mat with another towel. The driver stood to the side, muttering to himself.

Alicia was so embarrassed, but this was life with children. Trav walked to a nearby trash can and threw the towels away. She looked up. They were only twenty feet from the parking lot of the beach. If only they could've made it.

"You okay, bud?" She pushed the hair away from Preston's head.

"Yeah, I feel lots better. Can we go swim in the ocean?"

Trav chuckled. "Might be the best way to clean you up."

Alicia laughed with him. He'd handled all of this like a champ. He didn't deal with Preston on a daily basis and she'd wrongfully assumed that he was so successful and wealthy now that a little throw-up would disgust him. Even if she could never be married to a race car driver again, she still thought Trav was an amazing dad.

Trav turned to the driver. "I'm sorry. Do you want me to pay you now?"

"Yes. I don't want sick boy in my cab."

Trav arched an eyebrow at Alicia and pulled out his money clip. "How much?"

"Three hundred and fifty American."

Both eyebrows went up. "For an hour drive?"

"Clean my car."

Trav pulled out a wad of cash and his brow squiggled. He handed over three hundred-dollar bills, a twenty, and a few dollars. "Sorry, man, this is all I have. Do you take credit cards?"

"No, I don't!"

Alicia laughed. She couldn't help it.

Trav started laughing too, and pointed at her. "I'm trying to honor your wishes of middle-class and left most of my cash in the safe."

She pulled a small purse out of her beach bag and handed over fifty dollars. The cab driver looked at them like they were nuts, but climbed in and drove off.

"I kind of get the impression he's not a fan," Alicia said.

Trav grinned. "Now that would be a first for me."

"I'm sure it would. I was waiting for you to offer him driving lessons."

"Seriously! No wonder Preston got sick. I was about to lose it myself." He winked at their son. "You sure you're feeling okay, bud? We can go back to the ship if you want to."

"I don't want to get in another car," Preston said.

"I don't blame you." He glanced at Alicia. "Shall we go play on the beach and then we'll figure it out?"

"Thanks, Dad!" Preston gave him a little hug. "Thank you, thank you!" He trooped off toward the beach. Alicia and Trav followed him through the dirt parking lot.

There were restaurants and stores lining the beach. Alicia bought them a few towels and a shovel and bucket for Preston, then gave one of the restaurant owners twenty bucks to rent chairs for the day. She could tell it was bugging Trav that she was paying for things.

They settled into the chairs and Preston started digging into the beautiful sand, having the time of his life. Alicia leaned back under the shade. This was really nice, now that they were here and not in that crazy cab.

The restaurant owner came and handed them each a piña colada and left a Sprite for Preston. Alicia reached for money, but he waved her off. "Part of the cost of chairs. Come see me when you get hungry."

"For sure. Thank you." She sipped the sweet drink, grinning at the pinched look on Trav's face. "Relax and enjoy."

He leaned back. "Sorry I don't have any money."

She laughed. "Stop being such a chauvinist. I don't care."

"I'm not being a chauvinist. I know you can provide well for yourself and Preston, but I invited you on this trip and I wanted to take care of everything."

Alicia couldn't resist touching his hand. He'd been so great through everything. "It's no problem, Trav. I appreciate you being a gentleman."

He rolled his eyes and watched Preston build a sand castle. "I feel like a real loser right now."

"You've never been more attractive to me." Her eyes widened and she clapped a hand over her mouth.

Trav's intent gaze made her feel warmer than the sun or humidity could dream of doing. He reached for her hand and pulled it away from her lips. "Guess you didn't mean for that to slip out."

"Not really." She let him hold her hand. It felt too good to pull away right now.

His thumb traced a pattern on the back of her hand. "Am I attractive to you?"

"Oh, Trav. That was never in question. I can't imagine anyone in the world being as attractive to me as you are."

"But yet you can never give me another chance for some reason."

She shook her head and pulled her hand free. "Trav, there are so many more important things than our attraction."

"Such as?"

"We are not getting into this right now." She focused on Preston and tried to let the gently rolling waves soothe her.

"When are we getting into this?" Trav asked quietly. "I've been waiting eight years to talk to you, Ally."

She couldn't help but look at his handsome, frustrated face. Had he really? She knew he cared about her and adored Preston, but he had such a different life, and though he had tried many times to get her to come with Preston or to make things work for them to get together, she assumed he was busy and fulfilled with the life he'd chosen. "Why didn't you ever come to the ranch?"

"What?" He drew back.

"All these years you claim you wanted to make it work, but yet you never came to find me at the ranch."

"Your mom didn't tell you?"

"Tell me what?" She sucked down more of the piña colada, needing something to get her through this conversation.

"I came when you had Preston."

"No. You came to the hospital." Which she appreciated, but he'd come to see his newborn son, not her.

"I came once you went home, too. Your mom told me in no uncertain terms that I wasn't welcome. A shotgun in my face, actually."

Sadly, she could imagine it too well.

"She wasn't going to let me break her girl's heart like Bill had done to her for all those years. She told me to respect your wishes to leave you alone and let you be happy." He flicked his thumb against his leg. "I shouldn't have listened to her. I mean, you'd already sent me divorce papers at that point and I was a mess without you, but I should've fought harder." His gaze flickered to Preston, then back to her face. "For both of you."

Her heart thumped uncontrollably as he stared at her, and her mind raced. Her mom had sent Trav packing because he was a race car driver and probably a womanizer just like her dad. Alicia was mad that she had never known Trav had come for her, but she understood why her mom had rushed to protect her from herself. She would've fallen for Trav if she saw him when she was all vulnerable after having Preston. Her dad had been a great guy to Carson and Alicia, but he'd hardly been there for her mom and Alicia had found out after he died that he'd always had a woman on the side. It made her sick to think of what her mom had been through.

After the horror of watching her dad die in a race car, she'd decided she couldn't watch her husband die the same way. When the tabloids splayed the pictures of Trav and his assistant, Holly, in compromising positions, she'd been done. She'd gone to his box at the Daytona 500, pregnant and probably irrational, ready to confront him. She still had hope that the tabloids were exaggerating and they could work it all out, but Holly had been waiting in his suite. The woman had explained exactly what was going on between them, with details thrown in that still made her stomach churn.

Alicia had flown back to Wyoming that night and Preston had been born a few weeks later. Trav had stayed at the hospital the entire time she'd been there with Preston as a newborn. Trav had been so great during that time. Even though she had sent him divorce papers that she was waiting on him to sign, she'd almost decided to give him another chance, no matter that she was torn apart at the thought of being a racer's wife, and she still had so many unanswered questions about Holly. There was so much to say right now, but was she ready to get into it?

"My mom was a mess, Trav. I'm sorry she turned you away."

He nodded. "I understand a little better now. Your dad was my idol, but I know he wasn't perfect."

"None of us are."

He smiled sadly at that. "True."

Preston jumped up. "Can we go try to body surf the waves?"

Trav and Alicia both stood. Trav touched her arm. "Can we talk more later?"

"Yes, but don't expect me to change my entire life, Trav. It's been too long."

They walked into the warm water after Preston, who was running ahead. "Too long for us?"

"Yes." She tried to make her voice firm.

Trav gave her a look that showed exactly why he was so successful at racing cars—determination, desire, and a refusal to quit. "We'll see."

CHAPTER NINE

Trav thought the beach day was great, but he was much more excited that he and Alicia were actually talking about something real. Maybe, just maybe, he could convince her to talk to him some more tonight.

After dinner they played shuffleboard. Preston was very insistent that it was a "family tradition." Trav had a hard time finding any fault with his son, but he noticed that Preston was really into doing things a certain way and he repeated certain phrases a lot.

After dinner, they went to a comedian that was one of the funniest acts Trav had ever seen. He didn't think Preston understood a lot of the jokes. They were clean, but a lot of them were making fun of television, music, and famous people from when Trav and Alicia were young. Trav's favorite part was listening to Alicia giggle. He hadn't heard her laugh like that in years.

They stood up after the show and Alicia wiped at her eyes. "I think I cried off all my makeup, laughing so hard."

"He was one of the funniest comedians I've ever heard. Should we grab some CDs?"

"For sure." She smiled at him, and when he offered his hand and she took it, Trav thought he was the luckiest guy in the world.

They bought a dozen CDs. The guy had told the crowd that the proceeds went to help children transitioning out of foster care at eighteen. Trav could give the CDs to his pit crew. They'd all love this guy's humor.

"Can we go get ice cream?" Preston asked.

"Sure," Trav said.

"We've probably had too much sugar," Alicia said.

"Oh, come on, it's vacation." Trav winked at her.

She shook her head, but didn't complain as they walked through the promenade to Ben & Jerry's.

While Preston looked over all the flavors, Trav held back and squeezed Alicia's hand. "Sorry. I shouldn't have overruled you back there. I just really wanted ice cream."

"It's okay. It's not about the ice cream. I was just trying to make sure he's not creating a new rule. With shuffleboard and ..." Her voice trailed off and she looked at Trav apprehensively, almost fearfully.

"A new rule?" What in the world did that mean?

Preston had ordered cookies 'n cream and the girl was looking at them, waiting for their order. Alicia stepped forward and ordered chocolate with caramel sauce. Trav got a cone of cherry chip, handed over his ship card to the lady, and walked quietly back toward their suite. He kept sneaking glances at Alicia and Preston. He needed a week alone with her to talk out all their issues, but he'd just been given a huge clue that there were more issues with Preston. Those issues had to take precedence. He didn't care if he had to wait all night; she wasn't going to sleep until she talked to him.

Alicia sang Preston to sleep with a quavering voice. She knew Trav was waiting for her and she knew it wasn't going to be good, but it was time to share what was going on with Preston.

Preston was snoring lightly. She kissed his soft cheek, and her heart swelled with love. She couldn't imagine being more smitten with anyone, including Trav. It wasn't fair that Preston was struggling like he was, at such a young age, but there were worse problems out there and she thought Preston dealt with everything pretty well.

She stood on shaky legs and walked into the main area, shutting the door behind her. Trav glanced up from the couch, standing quickly. "We need to talk."

"Such an original line," she tried to tease.

He gave her half a smile, gesturing to the couch. She sat next to him and clasped her hands together.

"What rules were you talking about?" Trav asked.

Alicia exhaled. "Preston has OCD."

"What?" Trav exploded, rising out of his seat.

She waited until he settled down again. "I'm sorry I didn't tell you."

"Sorry?" Trav's voice went dangerously low. "How would you feel if I kept something like this from you?"

She knew he had every right to be angry, but his tone made her nervous. "It all started pretty recently, and it's not like you and I talk."

His mouth turned down. "When was he diagnosed?"

"A month ago."

"So tell me about it. What's going on?"

Alicia smiled. So Trav. Even if something was completely unjust and most people would hold on to anger or righteous indignation for a long time, Trav dealt with it and moved on. Probably one more reason he was so well-liked and successful.

"The therapist isn't sure why it manifested itself so young, but Preston's had a lot of hard things happen this year—not connecting with his teacher, not making the elite hockey team, he's really been missing you, his favorite horse died, and then Granny being diagnosed with breast cancer."

Trav nodded. "He's told me about most of that. I'm sorry about your mom."

She acknowledged that with a shrug. "It's tough, and he loves his Granny so much. The therapist said it's kind of like the perfect storm and even though he's so young, he's probably hitting a hormone surge because he's had a growth spurt. But it's really about him trying to do everything perfect." She lowered her voice. "To try to make us both proud. I think he assumes if he's perfect, we'll be a family again."

Trav's mouth tightened. "So this vacation and him wanting it to be perfect, you think it's all tied into that?"

"Probably." She exhaled, wringing her hands together. "My mom and I started noticing right after Christmas. He'd take hours on his homework, erasing until he had a hole in the paper. Then it was about his socks being put on perfectly; it could take him half an hour to get them right. Then he started having to shut doors a certain way. I thought I was living with Rain Man."

Trav's eyes were wide. He shook his head and looked down at his clasped hands. He looked broken, this tough man who excelled at his career and was so well-loved by the media. She still watched his every race, though no one but she and Preston knew that. His son's mental illness was obviously ripping him apart.

"He's doing really well," Alicia hastened to reassure him. "He never had to take medication; we just try to eat healthy and keep up on his vitamins. He's broken all the 'rules' he's made for himself, like the socks, doors, and writing perfect. His therapist told me the last time we were there that he only needed to come in a couple more times. She's really happy with his progress, but she warned me we'll need to start therapy again once he does hit puberty. That's when most youth have something like this manifest."

"Okay."

He was so understanding, so kind. Alicia wished he would say more so she wouldn't keep talking, but he just looked at her compassionately. She wrapped her arms around herself. "The last time we met with the therapist, I kept thinking, 'This kid doesn't need counseling, he needs a mom who's there. Needs to come in from school and have a snack waiting and Mom doing homework with him, talking about his day and how to deal with crap.' I feel like I'm failing."

"Aw, Ally. You can't take all of this on yourself. You're a single mom." He pushed a hand through his hair. "I hate that you're a single mom."

She smiled sadly at him. "It is what it is. Thanks for listening."

Trav blinked at her. "Ally. I always want to know about everything with Preston. I also want to know everything about you."

Alicia's stomach tightened. It was hard enough to talk about

Preston; she wasn't ready to hash out her and Trav's past. Tears streaked down her face. "Sometimes I feel like such an awful mother. How can I keep up with my practice, the ranch, and be there for Preston? Plus, I'm running my mom to chemo and radiation when Carson can't. It's so hard watching her be miserable."

"I'm sorry." Trav gathered her in his arms.

She didn't resist, but laid her head against his chest, feeling not just the strength of his muscles but the strength of his soul. Trav was good, through and through. If only she could rely on him all the time. She'd missed his strong chest and his warm, sexy smell, and his kiss ... Okay, she needed to stop these thoughts now.

He held her for several wonderful minutes as the tears fell. "You're a fabulous mom. I see the way Preston looks at you. The love you two share." Trav kissed her forehead. "I don't know how you do it all, but I've never once doubted that Preston was well taken care of and loved. Knowing that is the only way I've been able to handle not being with him more."

"Thanks, Trav." He wasn't just blowing sunshine. Even as kind as Trav was, he didn't do that. She gazed up at him, and her body acted on its own accord as she arched up and pressed her lips to his.

Trav tightened his arms around her, returning the kiss without hesitation. His lips were warm, demanding, and wonderful. Alicia wrapped her arms around his neck and pulled him in tighter. Trav easily lifted her onto his lap and intensified the kiss. Her lips parted and they became one. Alicia's body was on fire. Everywhere Trav touched made her want more and more.

Her head was cloudy with desire, but she forced herself to pull back and grasp his face between her hands. "Trav."

"Yes?" His voice was raw and low.

"We have to stop."

"Why?" He pulled her in and buried his face in her neck.

Alicia racked her brains for the reason, mostly because she was getting out of control and making out with her ex was a recipe for disaster. Her mind kept slipping back to how things had been between them when they were married. Why did she have to still love him?

"I ... have a boyfriend." She said the one thing she probably shouldn't have said.

Trav's head whipped up. His hands loosened on her waist and he stared at her like she'd stabbed his dog. Several awful seconds passed before he said, "Now that kind of talk during kissing is extremely inappropriate."

Alicia couldn't help but laugh. She pushed to her feet.

Trav stood with her. "Wait a minute. You're ending that brilliant performance with a lame excuse about a boyfriend I haven't heard wind of before this moment?"

"It-it's not a lame excuse." She stood straighter. "I really do have a boyfriend, and I shouldn't be like this with you."

"So it's pretty serious?" Trav looked almost as angry as when he'd found out about Preston.

"Even if it wasn't, I can't be like this with you."

"Why not?"

Alicia studied him and swallowed. "I would never be with a race car driver again."

His eyes darkened. "So I have to choose between my car and my family?"

"You chose your car long ago, Trav." She walked to her room quickly, hoping he wouldn't respond.

"You never gave me a choice."

She shut the door and pretended she hadn't heard him. If only she really hadn't. Had she really taken all his choice away, leaving like she did? He was right. She'd never given him a choice, because she reasoned that she couldn't do that to him. He was born to race and it was wrong of her to not support him in his dreams and passions. Only her mom truly understood.

But the deeper truth was ... she didn't ever give him the choice because she didn't want to know what his answer would've been.

CHAPTER TEN

Alicia slipped from her room and out the suite's main door when she heard Trav's shower start up. She carried her ship card and a water bottle off the ship and onto the rocky shores of St. Kitts, smiling at the workers. Before she reached the end of the dock, she broke into a run. She'd hoped there would be a beach to run on, but it was all shops and city. She pounded through the city streets, which were already busy with traffic. She missed running at home in the empty back roads of Alpine. She especially missed running the trails in the mountains.

She'd hardly slept, beating herself up for kissing Trav and then walking away from him. He was right that Duke wasn't much of a boyfriend if she'd hardly thought of him this week, only bringing him up when she needed an excuse to stay away from Trav.

There were so many issues with her and Trav. Many of them were in her head, but she didn't know how to cure them. Maybe she was the one that needed counseling, not Preston. Her dad's death had flipped her out. Yes, it had been terrifying to watch her personal hero die in a race car, but it had only gotten worse when her mom broke down and told her all about the affairs and the race car lifestyle her dad had lived when he wasn't with them. Why her mom put up with it, Alicia could never understand. It had seemed like fate when she'd seen the tabloid pictures of Holly and Trav not long after that. Then she'd gone to his race and Holly had told her all the sordid details of their affair and confirmed every one of Alicia's fears.

Alicia shook her head. She needed to think about something else, like maybe where in the world she was. She stopped and glanced around at the street. Some men were lounging in front of a run-down house, and they were eyeing her. When they saw she was looking at them, one of them stood and started toward her. Alicia had no clue if they were friend or foe, but she didn't wait around to find out. She turned on her heel and took off back the way she'd come, almost in an all-out sprint.

Glancing over her shoulder, she saw the man gesturing to her and running to keep up. Alicia kicked up her speed even higher, gasping for breath. She'd crossed several blocks before she dared look back again. The man was gone. Dragging in long gulps of air, she paused to catch her breath and get her bearings.

Over the top of the buildings she could see the spires of the cruise ships. She forced herself back into a jog and weaved through the streets, always keeping an eye on the ships. It was over an hour later when she trudged into the suite.

Trav ran out of his room, clutching a small athletic bag.

Preston was lying on the sofa, watching a cartoon on the television. "Hi, Momma."

"Hey, buddy. Sorry I took so long."

"It's okay. I ate bacon and me and Daddy explored the ship for a while." He sat up and grinned. "Dad says we're going to swim with dolphins today!"

"I can't wait. I'll go get showered and ready." She glanced at Trav.

He was staring at her with frightening intensity. She gave him what she hoped was a smile and hurried to her room, swinging the door shut. Trav's hand stopped the door from shutting completely and he followed her into her room.

"Sorry," she said weakly. "I lost track of time."

He took a long breath, then closed his eyes, his hands gripped into tight fists. When he opened his eyes, she was ready for a tongue-lashing; her brother and dad would definitely have given her one. "Can you please let me know where you're going next time and take your phone with you?"

She swallowed and nodded. "I didn't mean to make you worry."

His eyes swept over her. "I know. I just want to know you're safe." He pushed a hand through his hair. "When you'd been gone an hour and a half, I woke Preston up, grabbed him a pile of bacon from the buffet, and made him look all over the ship for you. Then I checked with security and they'd shown that you'd gotten off the ship. We came back here to gather stuff up so we could get off the ship and try to find you." He shook his head. "I was scared, Ally."

She smiled weakly, wishing she could just hug him, but after last night she needed to avoid sending him all these mixed signals. "I'm sorry," she muttered again.

He took two steps toward her and pulled her into his arms. She had to stink from sweating in all that humidity and running for over two hours, but he didn't seem to mind and she couldn't complain when he held her like this. "I want you with me always, Ally," he whispered into her hair. "I want to be there for you and protect you."

Alicia closed her eyes and wrapped her arms around his strong back. How was she supposed to respond to that? She never wanted to be apart from him, but his career, his relationship with Holly and who knew what other women, and her fears of watching him die in a car made that impossible. When too many seconds passed without her saying anything, he dropped his arms and backed away.

Alicia gave him another wan smile and muttered, "I'll get ready quick so we aren't late."

She grabbed a swimsuit from the drawer and hurried into the bathroom, unable to look him in the eye.

Trav stood on the raised concrete platform under the water at the dolphin push, pull, and swim on St. Kitts. He was about chest deep and watching a teenage girl hold on to a dolphin's fins and get pulled through the water. He imagined the excursion would be fun, if he wasn't so morose. It looked like Preston and Alicia were having fun, and it was interesting to touch the smooth skin of the dolphin as it played with the group and to have the dolphin push his foot while he held on to a boogie board or grabbed the dolphin's fins and it swam him around.

It was all good, so why was he so miserable? Maybe it was the annoying family from Wisconsin who'd recognized him earlier in the week, and got put in their group of ten for the excursion. The dad wanted to talk cars with him the entire time, even though right now he couldn't care less about cars, and the teenage daughter kept giving him longing looks that he ignored. Maybe it was because he was sunburned from the beach yesterday. Maybe it was because he didn't eat breakfast, too consumed with finding his wife—or rather, ex-wife.

He glanced over at the beauty, standing on the underwater platform next to him. Even with a life jacket on, he could still see glimpses of her beautiful figure in a two-piece swimsuit. But it wasn't just Alicia's beauty that held him captive. He'd dated plenty of beautiful women over the past eight years. It was her devotion to Preston, her kindness to everyone around her, her intellect, her sense of humor, and the fact that he had always been hopelessly in love with her.

He pulled his gaze away and focused on Preston, who had swum out with the kickboard and was waiting for his turn for the dolphin to push him in. He had a smile on, but he looked nervous.

"You'll do great, bud," Trav called out. "Just keep your legs straight."

The mom from Wisconsin sighed. "He's such a good dad," she whispered loudly to her daughter.

"And stinking hot." The daughter winked at him.

Trav ignored both of them.

"Oh my, lame race car groupies," Alicia muttered.

Trav shot her a look. It wouldn't hurt if she was a little bit of a race car groupie, but he kind of liked the jealous tone in her voice.

The dolphin reached Preston and within moments he was shooting across the water toward them as if a giant wave was pushing him. Preston had a grin a mile wide. He landed on the raised step and handed the board off to the instructor. "Thank you, sir, that was awesome!"

The guy ruffled his hair. "You did great, bud."

Preston pushed through the water along the walkway to where Trav and Alicia stood.

"You were amazing," Alicia said. "Did you love it?"

"It was so fun, Mom!" He grabbed Trav and squeezed him tight. "Thank you, Dad. Thank you, thank you! This is the best family vacation, ever!"

"I thought they were divorced," the teenager from Wisconsin said loudly.

Trav hugged his son, unable to resist glancing at Alicia. Yes, they were divorced, but they were still a family of sorts. It was surreal to him that people all over the nation bought a certain kind of cologne if he said he wore it, and he was idolized for his skill in a race car, his money, and influence, yet he couldn't influence or buy the one thing he wanted—Alicia.

"Your turn for a kiss, pretty lady." The guide motioned to Alicia. "Now put your hands on top of each other, palms up."

The dolphin swam up to Alicia and she bent down and gently kissed his nose, then turned her head to the side and let him kiss her cheek. She let out the cutest giggle.

"Best kiss you've ever had, eh, Mum?" The guide winked at her.

Alicia cast a glance at Trav. "Not even close."

The entire group laughed at that, and the teenager from Wisconsin had to throw in, "I'd die for a kiss from Travis Poulsen."

Were his kisses something special, or was Alicia referring to her stupid cowboy boyfriend? He didn't have any proof the guy was a cowboy, but it would fit.

He went back to his Ally-induced stress haze and only snapped out of it when Ally stepped out of the pool in front of him and unstrapped her life jacket. Her golden-brown hair trailed down her back and her pink swimsuit highlighted her tanned skin and all of her features. Her exercising, riding horses, and busy lifestyle really had produced the most beautiful shape he'd ever seen, and he'd dated famous models and actresses. He swiped a hand over his face, relieved when Preston grabbed his hand. "Do we have time to go to the beach again, Dad?"

"You're up for another ride with a crazy cab driver?"

"I'll try to give Mom more warning if I throw up this time." Preston laughed.

Trav squeezed his son's hand, exchanging a smile with Ally as they walked to the shop where they could view their dolphin excursion pictures. Tomorrow was their last full day on the ship. Trav didn't want this time to end, but at the same time he didn't know how much longer he could take this ping-pong with Ally. Nothing he said or did seemed to change her mind about race car drivers. He loved his career, it was his life, but he would most likely give it all up if Ally asked him to. Like he'd told her last night, though, she'd never asked. He didn't know if she ever would. Maybe it had nothing to do with his career; maybe he just wasn't enough for her.

CHAPTER ELEVEN

Their last sea day flew by with doing the flow rider, playing miniature golf, swimming in all the pools and trying out every waterslide, and eating far too much. Alicia would always treasure these memories with Trav and Preston, but being so close to her ex-husband had about ripped her apart emotionally. She would be sad when they docked in Fort Lauderdale tomorrow, but it was time to get back home and figure out how to cut back her work hours, be there for Preston more, and help her mom deal with her treatments and fight through the cancer. Trav would have to go back to being a forbidden daydream. She frowned. It was a depressing thought.

They had proven throughout this week together that they could be civil, more than civil when they were kissing. She sighed at the thought.

She could come with Preston to Trav's races, or maybe they could even do another vacation. Not Kauai like he suggested, but boogie boarding in California would be nice.

At dinner they took lots of pictures with Chakib and Mayara, and Preston had to give Mayara a kiss on the cheek and tell her he loved her. It was adorable.

They'd planned to go for a night swim after dinner, but Preston clutched his stomach as they neared their room. "I don't feel so good," he moaned.

Trav threw a concerned look at Alicia and hurried Preston to his bathroom. Preston promptly threw up, luckily in the toilet. Alicia helped him take a shower, put on pajamas, and get settled into his king-sized bed. He was pale and sweaty.

"Do you think you ate too much?" Trav asked.

"I don't know." Preston groaned. "My stomach kills." He grasped the right side of his abdomen.

Alicia knelt next to him on the bed, Trav at her side. She gently touched Preston's stomach. "Just on the right?"

He nodded. "It started in the middle, but now it's moved."

"When did it start?"

"When we were swimming before dinner."

"Why didn't you tell us?"

"I didn't want to ruin our last day of being a family."

Alicia exchanged a glance with Trav. Her heart broke for her little boy. He recognized this wasn't going to continue and he didn't want to miss out on a second.

She jumped from the bed, hurried to her room, and found the children's Tylenol. She rushed back and gave Preston a dose, and Trav offered him a cold water bottle. Preston sucked some down and curled into a ball on the bed, holding his stomach.

Alicia was starting to get scared. Preston was warm to the touch and looked so pale. The flu wouldn't usually come on this quickly and it might be food poisoning, but he'd been hurting earlier and still had eaten dinner. He wouldn't have a fever with food poisoning, right? Something wasn't adding up.

"I'm calling the ship's doc," Trav said, reaching for the phone next to the bed.

"Thanks," Alicia whispered. She hardly paid attention to Trav's description of the illness as she got a cold washcloth and placed it to Preston's forehead.

"It hurts," Preston murmured.

Alicia gently held the washcloth with one hand and rubbed his back with the other. "Daddy's getting some help. You'll be okay, sweetie."

"Pray for me, Momma," Preston begged.

Trav hung up the phone. "The doctor's on his way."

Tears formed in her eyes as she extended her hands to Trav. "He wants us to pray."

Trav nodded and clasped her hands. Alicia offered a short prayer, unable to stop the tears from spilling over.

Preston seemed a little calmer when she finished. "Thanks, Momma."

Alicia squeezed his hand and offered him another drink of water. He took a sip, but then vomited all over the bed, narrowly missing her.

"Oh, sweetie!" she cried out.

Trav ran for the bathroom, returning with a wet towel. He handed it to Alicia. She wiped up Preston, who was crying and grasping his stomach. Trav lifted the soiled bedding off, sliding Preston onto the clean sheets underneath, and bundled the blanket and top sheet into a pile in the far corner.

A rap came at the door. Trav hurried to answer it, returning with the doctor. He was close to their age, tall with thick blond hair, and had an Australian accent.

"Too much buffet?" he teased Preston.

Preston tried to smile, but then he was vomiting again. The doctor barely jumped out of the way. Trav grabbed a couple more clean towels and laid them over the mess while Alicia used the other end of the damp towel to wipe Preston's mouth.

"Possibly food poisoning?" the doctor mused. "Our ship is very safe. Did you eat out at St. Kitts?"

"We had a hamburger and fries on the beach."

He nodded and proceeded to check Preston's temperature and probe his abdomen. "He wouldn't have a temperature with food poisoning," he muttered, almost to himself. He spent a few more minutes, then stepped back. "You're a tough little guy. Are you okay if I talk to Mum and Papa for just a second?"

Preston nodded, but his eyes were wide and fearful. Alicia followed the doctor into the next room, with Trav trailing behind.

"He has appendicitis," the doctor said, wasting no time. "I have no facility to operate. We will call in Coast Guard and fly him to mainland. We are very close to mainland now."

Alicia swayed. Trav wrapped his arm around her waist, holding her up. "Now?" Trav asked.

"Right now." The doctor pulled a phone from his pocket and dialed, talking rapidly to what Alicia could only assume was the Coast Guard.

She could hardly stand upright. "What if his appendix bursts before they can get him to a hospital?" she whispered.

Trav squeezed her tight. "He'll be okay." He seemed to be reassuring himself.

The doctor hung up the phone. "Wrap him up in a clean blanket and Papa can carry him?" He glanced at Trav.

"For sure." Trav pulled a blanket from the closet. He gently helped Preston sit up, wrapped the blanket around him, and lifted him into his arms. Preston looked so small and frail against Trav's chest. Her little boy. Alicia had to press a fist to her mouth to hold a sob in.

The doctor led the way out of their suite. Alicia grabbed her purse and slipped into her shoes. Should she grab Trav's shoes and wallet? Would there be room in the helicopter for both of them? Was it fair if she insist she be the one to go with Preston? It was horrible to have to contemplate either of them being left behind. She scooped up Trav's flip-flops, figuring she had a credit card and insurance information in her purse. They could get all of their other stuff later ... if the Coast Guard let them both come.

She followed Trav and the doc down the hallway, across the pool area, and up a couple flights of steps onto the open deck above the pools. She hadn't even noticed there was an extra deck up here. Crew members were rapidly clearing the lounge chairs and tables out of the way. The wind whipped at her hair. It was vicious right now and she was surprised to see white caps on the water. A storm must be coming, but the ship was so big she hadn't noticed it rocking.

Trav hefted Preston a little higher and their son moaned. He looked like he was almost asleep. Hopefully the Tylenol she'd given him had taken away some of the pain and he could rest until he got to the hospital and had surgery. The doctor had said they weren't that far from the mainland.

She stood close to Trav as he held Preston and couldn't resist touching their son's soft cheek with her hand.

"He'll be okay," Trav said.

She tried to smile bravely, even though she wanted to just cuddle Preston and Trav close and bawl. They'd be to the hospital soon, and then after surgery they could all be together.

The steady thrum of helicopter blades cut through the evening air. Alicia's stomach jumped. Within seconds she could see the lights of the helicopter. It looked big, big enough to fit all of them. What a relief.

One of the men—she thought he might be the ship's captain with all the braids on the shoulders of his uniform—was speaking rapidly into a phone. He turned to them with a sober expression. "There's no room to land a bird that big on this ship. They will drop a basket for your son."

"A ... what?" Alicia probably shrieked the words. They weren't landing the helicopter so their family could climb safely in? She'd envisioned herself and Trav holding Preston throughout the ride, praying and singing to him. She didn't love heights any more than Preston did. How would it work for them to both ride up in a basket? Her stomach tumbled just imagining it, but she'd do anything to stay by Preston's side. Would Trav be okay left behind? That was such an awful thought. She wouldn't be okay. Their eyes met over Preston's head and she could see the battle he was facing.

"If only one of us can go ... I'll stay," he said.

"Oh, Trav." Alicia crumpled at his kindness. Her shoulders rounded and tears raced down her face. She knew he wanted to be with Preston every bit as much as she did, but he was willing to sacrifice ... for her. *Please, Lord. Let them be able to fit both of us.*

The chopper was directly above them now, staying away from the large smokestacks of the ship. She wondered how in the world the pilot kept it from crashing with the moving ship and all the wind. She and Preston were going to be riding in that unstable-looking chopper. Her stomach plummeted. *Oh, please help us, Lord.*

A basket descended, with a man holding on to the side of it. It was agonizing to watch the man and the basket whip in the wind. Would she have to hold on like that man was doing? There definitely wasn't room in the basket for more than one person. Her palms were sweating and acid climbed her throat. *For Preston. For Preston.*

The basket and the man finally reached the deck. Wind whipped her hair into her face. The loud thump-thump of the helicopter rotors made it hard to hear or think. Everybody was coiled for action and stressed, or maybe it was simply her stress radiating off of them.

The Coast Guard guy motioned to Trav. "Let's go!"

Alicia hurried by his side as Trav settled Preston into the basket and kissed his forehead. "Love you, bud."

Preston's eyes flew open as Trav stepped back and the Coast Guard guy quickly strapped their son in. "Dad? Mom?"

Alicia bent down as close as she could without getting in the way. "I'm here, sweetie."

She glanced up at Trav, feeling so horrible that they were going to leave him behind. Tears stained his tanned face. She could never thank him enough for allowing her to go.

"Kiss him goodbye, Momma," the Coast Guard guy instructed, stepping back into his spot, clipping some kind of bracket into place that was also attached to his waist, and grasping the ropes.

"Kiss him ... no! I'm going with you." Alicia stepped up onto the other side of the basket, and grasped the ropes just like he was doing.

"No." His eyes widened as he shook his head. "Step down."

"No!' Alicia yelled.

The guy motioned frantically to some of the cruise ship crew. "We've got to go!"

Alicia looked down at her son, her heart beating out of control.

"Momma," he whispered. She could barely hear him above the whir of the helicopter blades and the gusts of wind. His hand lifted toward her.

Hands grabbed her around the waist and tugged her. "No!" she screamed. She grasped at the ropes with everything she had.

"Momma!" Preston screamed. His little face convulsed in pain. He gripped his stomach as tears ran down his face. "Momma!"

Somebody ripped her right hand off the rope. Alicia screamed and elbowed them, clinging with her left hand. They couldn't do this to her. They couldn't take her boy without her.

"Stop!" Trav cried out. He dodged around one crew member, but two more grabbed him from behind, slowing his progress to her.

"Trav!" she screamed.

Two men had her waist and right arm, and someone else pried her fingers off the rope. "You're endangering everyone!" someone yelled at her.

Preston was shrieking, "Momma!"

"Preston!" Alicia screamed.

The Coast Guard guy yelled something she couldn't decipher and the basket lifted up into the air, swaying and bobbing with the wind. Preston's cries for her were carried away, growing fainter and fainter until they intermingled with the chopper's blades.

Alicia stopped fighting and went limp. The men were holding her up as she sobbed. "Preston. Trav."

"Let go of her!" Trav yelled.

The men transferred her to Trav's arms. She sank into him, crying so hard her head throbbed with the pressure of it. She turned her face up to watch the basket disappear into the helicopter; the doors shut, and they streaked off into the night.

The crew members apologized for their rough treatment, and someone tried to explain how precarious the helicopter had been. The doctor said the severity of Preston's condition meant they needed to get him to a hospital quickly. Alicia didn't acknowledge any of it. She simply clung to Trav and bawled. They'd taken her son. What if his appendix burst on the way and they lost him? She hadn't even had a chance to kiss him goodbye or tell him how much she loved him.

His shrieks for her bounced around in her mind. He had to be terrified, and he was in so much pain. He needed his momma.

Trav held her tightly. He was the rock she needed right now.

"What can we do to help?" the captain guy asked, and it was the first thing from any of them she wanted to respond to. What could anyone do to help besides get her and Trav to Preston's side?

"We need to call my brother. Somebody needs to meet him at the hospital." She wished her mom could go, but her health just wasn't there.

Trav kissed her forehead. "I left my phone in the room."

The captain handed over his phone. Alicia had to think for a minute. Her brain was so scrambled and she had Carson's number programmed in, so she rarely dialed it. Finally it came to her: 970-920-8776.

Carson didn't answer. No! It would be early evening. Was he out doing chores and couldn't hear the phone? Did he think it was a telemarketer? She left a hurried message, explaining the situation and asking him to fly to Miami as quickly as possible.

As she hung up the phone, despair overwhelmed her. "Even if he gets this and finds a flight leaving soon, it'll be hours before he gets there."

Trav took the phone from her, determination glinting in his eyes. He dialed a number.

"Who are you calling?"

"Holly."

Alicia stiffened. She didn't want that woman anywhere near her son, filling in for her with Preston like she'd filled in for Alicia with Trav. How could he be so insensitive? Then shame rushed through her. He'd been willing to stay behind when they thought she was going with Preston. He was trying to help their son. She had to get over her issues right now.

She released her grip on Trav and he gave her a questioning glance, but Holly must've answered right then. Alicia listened numbly as Trav explained the situation, clarifying with the captain that Preston would probably be taken to Miami Children's Hospital, and then thanking her before ending the call and handing the phone to the captain.

The thought of Holly had actually calmed Alicia down. Tears still trailed down her face and her body was shaking, but she didn't feel so out of control as she had when she'd watched them take her boy away. She didn't like Holly, but at least someone who was familiar would be there with Preston. Her boy. She couldn't stop thinking about how scared he must be. How long of a flight was it? Did the Coast Guard have medicine to numb the pain? Did they have an experienced medic who could keep her boy alive if he took a turn for the worse and his appendix actually burst? She pressed her hand to her mouth.

Trav wrapped his arm around her waist and tugged her close. Even though she hated the reminder of Holly coming between them, she couldn't resist holding on to him and sobbing against his chest. He didn't offer any empty reassurances, but simply held her.

The men quietly walked away, except for the captain. Alicia didn't have the strength to even look at him as he spoke. "We will be in Fort Lauderdale by four-thirty tomorrow morning and you will be the first people off the ship. I will send a specialist by your cabin who will upload your passports and take care of everything with customs."

"Thank you." Trav took a deep breath that Alicia could feel. "Is there any way for us to get off the ship faster?"

"A private helicopter might have the range to reach us in the next few hours and fly you back."

"I'll have my assistant coordinate that," Trav said.

"Is her phone number the last one you spoke with?"

"Yes."

"I'll contact her with some suggestions of companies and give her my direct number so we can stay in touch with coordinates."

"Thank you." Trav nudged Alicia toward the stairs. "Let's get you down to our room."

Alicia was so numb, it was all she could do to nod.

"Everyone will be praying for you and your son, ma'am," the captain said.

"Thank you," she mumbled.

Trav kept his arm around her and they walked slowly across the deck and down the stairs. They were in the hallway by their room when an announcement blared over the loud speakers. "Many of you probably noticed the Coast Guard helicopter dropping a basket over Deck Fourteen a few minutes ago. One of our young guests has developed appendicitis and it was necessary to fly him to a hospital as soon as possible. Please, whatever your religious affiliation, say a prayer or give positive energy toward Preston Noir and his parents. God bless."

Alicia sagged against Trav. She truly appreciated the thought and knew the strength of other's prayers would help. Trav pulled a key card out of his pocket and slid it in. He escorted her through the room and eased her down onto the couch.

Alicia wanted to be strong, to help Trav like he was helping her, but she could barely stay upright as her mind whirred with fears for Preston and worries over how he was feeling—physically and emotionally. She was gone so much he craved her attention, and now, when he needed her most, she couldn't be there.

"I'm sorry I'm such a mess," she muttered.

"Oh, Ally." Trav cradled her face with his palm. "I'd worry if you weren't a mess. Watching them pull you away from Pres—" His voice broke and he gathered her close again.

Alicia clung to him, resting her cheek against his shoulder and allowing the tears to just fall. Trav had been so strong and he deserved to cry for as long as he wanted. This was the most horrible thing she'd ever experienced, but having Trav close made it bearable.

Trav's phone rang and an automated voice said, "Holly Dresden, assistant extraordinaire."

"I better talk to her about the helicopter."

Alicia released him. "Please do. That would be such a blessing to get there sooner."

Trav stood, and a chill swept over Alicia as she half-listened to Trav coordinating things with Holly. She wrapped her arms around herself, but it didn't help much.

Then it hit her she should try Carson again, or her mom. She called him, and his voice was scratchy. "Hello?"

"Cars! Did you get my message?"

"Yes." He cleared his throat, but it didn't sound much better. "Sorry, I've got strep throat."

"Oh no. Don't come."

"I'm coming. I found a flight out of Jackson Hole that leaves tomorrow morning at six."

"We'll be to him before that. Trav's assistant is going to be with him now and we're getting a chopper to come get us."

"I want to be there for him."

"I know, but if you're contagious there's no way they'll let you into the hospital. Stay home and rest and I'll get a hold of you when I know something. Let Mom know what's going on. Ask her to pray." Her mom's prayers turned sour milk into ice cream.

"Okay." His voice sounded so ouchy. "You okay?"

"I'm a basket case, but Trav's here, so that helps." She glanced up to see that Trav had ended his call and was watching her.

"Oh? Guess the cruise went as well as he'd hoped."

"No, nothing like that. I'll talk to you soon."

"Okay. I can take a hint. Mom and I will be praying for Preston."

"Thanks." The tears started coming again. Would they ever stop?

Carson hung up and Trav started toward her, but a sharp rap on the door stopped him. He hurried over and swung the door open. Drew, their buddy from Jamaica, had a cart piled with food and drinks.

"Sorry, mon." His eyes swung to Alicia. "Sorry, Mum. You probably don't want to eat anything, but I wanted to do something."

"Thank you," Alicia said, brushing her tears away.

Drew wheeled the cart in and deposited everything on the table quickly. He nodded to Alicia and shook Trav's hand as he left.

Trav pushed a hand through his hair. "Good guy."

Alicia focused on him. "So are you."

He quirked a smile. "What do you want to do? Eat?"

"No. Not really." How did she tell him the only thing that would help was for him to hold her while they waited for news? She felt apprehensive, but forced herself to whisper, "Could we just ... be together?"

Trav nodded, his eyes full of questions and concerns. Alicia wondered if he'd want to talk, and knew she wasn't in any sane frame of mind. If he asked her right at this moment to be a family again, she'd probably say yes. He meant so much to her.

He sank down on the couch and gingerly wrapped his arm around her shoulder. Alicia sank into him, laying her head against his chest.

"You're probably exhausted," he said.

When he said that, she realized he was right. The adrenaline had left, but the overwhelming fear was still there. She didn't know how to talk about Preston without breaking down. "Can we pray together?"

"Of course." Instead of kneeling, Trav wrapped both arms around her and started praying.

Alicia listened to the deep rumble of his voice and felt the first sense of peace she'd had tonight. It was simple, but so heartfelt, and when his voice cracked on the words, "Please, Lord, protect our boy," she realized how good Trav was, through and through. She doubted everything at the moment—Trav ever being with Holly, her own choice to walk away from the racing circuit, if Preston was going to be okay. It all hurt and terrified her, but Trav's faith and strength buoyed her up so she could have faith and trust in God, even if she wasn't in control. An appendix had flipped her world just as much as her father's death and Trav's race car. Could she let go of the safe yet incomplete life she'd built for her and Preston and trust Trav and the Lord?

CHAPTER TWELVE

Trav lifted his feet onto the ottoman, leaning back into the couch and cradling Ally closer. They hadn't said much after the prayer, and he thought it was probably for the best that she'd drifted off to sleep. But that would leave him alone with his thoughts until the chopper came, and he didn't like his thoughts right now.

The terror for Preston's health and safety drummed through his mind, giving him a tension headache. How close was he to the hospital? What if his appendix burst? Trav scrubbed a hand over his face. It was horrific that neither he or Alicia could be there to comfort or watch over him. Trav hadn't wanted to sacrifice and stay behind, but he was willing to do it for Alicia and Preston. A boy needed his mom at moments like that. But when they'd both realized Alicia couldn't go and he'd had to watch those men pull Alicia away from the ropes, he had flipped out and gotten uncharacteristically violent trying to fight his way to Ally. He'd wanted to fight them all, do something crazy like unhook the Coast Guard guy and hook Alicia in, but Preston's safety overrode any heroic or unheroic tendencies.

He glanced down at Alicia's beautiful face. She was such a great mom. It killed him how she beat herself up. It was honestly little wonder Preston had OCD, because Alicia had always had those tendencies. Not that he blamed her. The drive to perfection had made her a successful lawyer and a wonderful mother and kept her in unreal physical condition, but she was always so hard on herself.

He laid his head back against the couch, a nonstop prayer for Preston and Alicia rolling through his head. He'd do anything for them. He closed his eyes. Well, almost anything. If Alicia would've asked him eight years ago to quit racing, would he have? No way, no how. And he had to respect her for never asking. Of course there'd been other issues, too, with her believing stupid tabloid pictures over her own husband, but he knew it all came down to her dad putting the car before his family and her worry that Trav would do the same. Her dad dying on the track had been horrific for both of them, and instead of coming together and talking through their fears, they'd split apart.

He couldn't claim he wasn't scared sometimes, but he was at the peak of his career right now. Could he walk away? Did she want him to? He didn't have any answers, but one thing was certain: he wasn't letting Preston or Alicia walk away without a battle. He'd put up a weak resistance last time, but he'd given up when her mom had convinced him that Alicia was better off without him and his lifestyle. This week he'd had a glimpse of what their family could be, and the only person who could truly take that from him was lying in his arms right now. He loved her so much. If only he could find a way to make her love him back.

The cabin phone rang. Alicia jumped and grabbed his arm. "Preston!" Her eyes were wild and unfocused.

"It's okay, sweetheart. We'll be with him soon." He reached over and grabbed the phone.

"Mr. Poulsen. The helicopter should be here within twenty minutes if you want to gather up a small bag of supplies and meet us at Deck Fourteen. We will pack up your other belongings and get them to you after we dock."

"We'll be right there. Thank you." Relief pulsed through him. He hung up and couldn't resist giving Alicia a hug and a quick peck on the lips. "The helicopter will be here in twenty minutes."

Alicia jumped to her feet, running for her shoes and purse. She was at the door before Trav had done much more than stand. "I need to open the safe and get a few things," he said.

"Well, hurry up, our boy is waiting!" She actually smiled.

Trav returned the smile, grateful her optimism had been restored. He wished the captain would've told him news on Preston, but maybe they didn't have any yet.

He strode to his bedroom, opened the safe, and quickly grabbed his wallet, the cash he'd stashed in the safe, and his passport. He stopped by the trays of food from room service. Drew was such a great guy. There was a pad of paper and a pen on the side table. He wrote a quick thank-you and placed a couple hundred-dollar bills on it.

Alicia watched him, smiling her approval. He held open the door for her and took her hand as they entered the hallway. She squeezed his hand in response.

"Are you feeling a little better?" he asked.

"Yes. It helps so much knowing we're on our way to him. I'm still freaking out with worry, but I feel a lot of peace too, if that makes any sense. Sorry I fell asleep on you."

"You can sleep on me anytime, darlin'."

Alicia laughed. "Is that a solid offer, cowboy?"

"Yes, ma'am." Trav squeezed her hand and escorted her up the stairs. There was no way he was letting her and Preston go.

CHAPTER THIRTEEN

Trav and Alicia burst into the emergency room waiting area. Holly stood and hurried to them. She was just as beautiful as Alicia remembered—sleek blonde hair, long legs, bright red lipstick. She gave Trav a quick hug. Her eyes darted to Alicia, then away. "I haven't even seen him yet. They ... oh, Trav, the appendix burst. I think it's bad!"

Alicia swayed on her feet. Why hadn't someone told them? Trav turned to her and gathered her into his arms. Holly moved toward the wall and stood, wringing her hands together and watching them. Alicia closed her eyes and buried her face in Trav's chest. Preston, oh, Preston.

"Can't that kill him?" she whispered against Trav.

"He's here at the hospital. That's a good thing, right?"

Tears wet his shirt. Her body shook. They finally made it here and Preston wasn't doing good.

A receptionist watched them from her desk. Alicia straightened her spine, pulled from Trav's arms, and marched over to her. "My son is Preston Noir. I need to know what's going on with him."

"Yes, ma'am." The lady picked up the phone and dialed quick, muttering and listening for a long minute before hanging up. Her eyes darted to Alicia, then away. "He's in surgery, ma'am. I'm sorry, but you'll have to wait for the doctor."

Trav came up and put his arm around her. "It's okay, Ally, he'll be okay."

"We don't know that." She sobbed and turned in to his embrace again, crying quietly against him as he held her and rubbed her back.

Holly appeared at Trav's side. "I've got to go," she told Trav. "Can you call me when he gets out of surgery?"

"Sure. Thank you."

"Of course. Anything for the boss man."

Alicia wanted to be jealous and petty and maybe rip a patch of Holly's hair out, but she was grateful for this woman's help with Preston and getting the helicopter for them to get here. "Th-thank you," she was able to get out.

Holly glanced at her, apprehension clouding her blue eyes. "It was the least I could do."

Alicia blinked, muddling through that response. The least she could do since she'd stolen Alicia's husband? Or was she talking about something else?

"Tell my cute buddy I'll bring him a present tomorrow."

"Will do. Thanks again."

Holly simply nodded, grabbed her purse, and was gone before Alicia could process why she was leaving so quickly. They didn't have a clue if Preston was okay or not. What if the worst happened? Did Holly not want to be here because of that? Was she uncomfortable seeing Trav hold Alicia?

"That was really kind of her," she muttered.

"She takes good care of me, that's for sure."

Alicia stared at him, wondering what in the world he could mean by that comment. Before she got a chance to ask, a doctor walked in the room. Alicia and Trav moved as one to intercept him.

"Excuse me," the doctor said. "Did a tall blonde just leave here? I have news about a boy in her charge."

"That was my assistant. I'm Trav Poulsen. Are you Preston's doctor?" Trav stuck out his hand.

Alicia just wanted to know that Preston was okay. Why was Trav dragging this out?

The doctor quickly shook his hand, then nodded to her. "You're Preston's parents?"

"Yes," Alicia hurried to respond. "I'm Alicia Noir."

The doctor smiled, and just the sight of it made Alicia's knees weak. He wouldn't be smiling if Preston wasn't all right. She leaned heavily into Trav.

"Dr. Cunningham. He's doing great. Caught the appendix just after it burst." He shook his head. "It was a mess. He'll be a little under the weather for a few days, but within a week you'll forget you even met me."

Trav smiled. "Thank you. You don't know what this means to us."

"Can we see him? Is he awake?" Alicia's voice trembled. She was so happy. Her boy! He was okay. She squeezed Trav and he squeezed back.

Dr. Cunningham grinned. "Follow me."

They hurried after him and Alicia thought the guy walked way too slow, but she was so happy she couldn't complain. She wanted to skip down the hallway, kiss Preston all over his cute little face, then kiss Trav all over his. She glanced at him, and he smiled and squeezed her hand.

The doctor led them through a set of double doors and down a hallway. "We'll move him to another room within the hour, but he should only have to stay until tomorrow night if everything looks good."

"How soon can we fly home?" Alicia asked.

Trav whipped around to look at her. Her eyes widened at the frustration in his gaze.

"Where's home?" the doctor asked.

"Wyoming," Alicia said.

"Boca Raton," Trav said.

The doctor arched his eyebrows. "I recommend Boca Raton for at least a few days; then he should do okay on a flight if you need to go back to Wyoming." He smiled at Alicia. "Sorry, but I'll take a fifty-minute drive over a six-hour plane ride." He paused at a door, pushed a curtain aside, and called out, "I brought a surprise, buddy."

"Oh yeah?" Preston's sweet little voice answered.

Alicia pushed around the doctor and was almost to her boy when the doctor grabbed her hand. "Slow down there, Momma, he did just have surgery."

"Okay." Alicia tugged her hand free, stopping at the side of Preston's bed and settling for reaching for his hand, then planting a kiss on each cheek.

"Hi, Momma," Preston whispered. "Hi, Dad."

Trav laid a hand on Preston's arm, then leaned down and kissed his forehead. "Hi, bud."

"Are you okay?" Alicia squeaked out. Her throat was so dry, and she was crying again. The anguish of the past six hours faded away. "Sorry, that was a dumb question. Of course you're not okay."

"My stomach feels a lot better."

"I'm so glad to hear that, sweetie."

"Dad?"

"Yeah, bud." Trav leaned in closer.

"When I'm feeling better, can we go on a helicopter ride?"

Trav gave a surprised chuckle and glanced at Alicia. "Um, sure."

"You really want to go on another helicopter ride?" she asked.

"Yeah." He looked exhausted and pale, but content. "I kept thinking it would be really fun if I didn't hurt so much. Maybe I'm not scared of heights anymore." His eyes drifted closed.

"I think he's going to recover just fine," the doctor said from behind them.

Alicia smiled. "Thank you. I think you're right."

CHAPTER FOURTEEN

After a couple of days at the hospital, they traveled the fifty minutes from Miami up the coast to Boca Raton. With their focus on Preston, things between her and Trav had been relaxed the three days they'd been home.

Trav's house was on Spanish River Road in Boca Raton. The river that flowed to the ocean was his backyard and the beach was only a couple blocks to the east. The house was unreal, more along the lines of a mansion. Alicia's favorite spot was the huge gathering area that included the kitchen, living room, and informal dining. It had three-story windows overlooking the green expanse of grass that made up the backyard and the peaceful river beyond. Every bedroom on the upper floor had its own bathroom and great views of the ocean to the east, and the basement housed a theater, a workout room, and a game room with pool, foosball, ping-pong, and arcade games.

Alicia felt like she was still on vacation with a maid service coming in and cleaning every morning and a delivery service bringing delicious dinners every night. She wasn't sure who stocked the pantry and fridge, but it was always done. Trav's life was very different from hers.

He'd worked out early every morning, then stayed with Preston while she went for long runs along the beach and the river, and then he'd go into work for a couple of hours. Alicia tried to catch up on work via email and phone calls in Trav's home office when Preston rested, but she was hopelessly behind. In the afternoon and evenings they kept Preston occupied with board games, books, and movies.

Alicia really enjoyed being here and appreciated that Trav hadn't pinned her down to any serious talks, but he'd taken any opportunity to touch her arm, brush against her, or give her a hug. They hadn't kissed again, and although she really wanted to, she knew it would mess both of them up even more. This life couldn't continue. She needed to get back to work and Preston needed to get back to school. Her mom and brother needed her also. Even though she loved Trav as much as ever, if not more, she was realizing that love might not be enough to overcome living across the country from each other and him still being dedicated to his race car. Plus they'd never talked about Holly, not that she really wanted to.

While Preston napped that afternoon, she responded to dozens of emails, then went to an online travel site and booked them a flight to Wyoming for the next morning.

Trav arrived home a few minutes later, and she hurriedly closed the screen, feeling guilty and not wanting to tell him yet.

They walked slowly to the beach, pushing Preston in the wheel-chair Trav had rented, and then they all sat in the sand and dug, listening to the waves. It was idyllic. How was she going to tell Trav they were leaving in the morning?

After a delicious dinner of chicken enchiladas and salad, they watched *The Princess Bride* and then settled Preston into bed.

"Good night, love." Alicia leaned down and kissed him. Trav had already given him a kiss and was waiting in the doorway.

"'Night," Preston whispered, already half asleep.

Alicia stood and walked to the doorway. She wished she could just grab on to Trav and hold on tight, but she had to be strong or she'd never get back to her life and let him get back to his. It had become pretty fuzzy over the past week and a half why she wanted to even do that.

"Momma?" Preston called out.

"Yes?" She turned in the doorway.

"Can we just stay with Daddy for always?"

Alicia sucked in a breath. She glanced at Trav, who was leaning toward her, a hopeful look on his handsome face. She looked away and admitted, "We're flying home in the morning."

"What?" Trav exploded.

"No, Momma!" Preston sat up too quickly, and it must've hurt his abdomen as he cried out in pain.

Alicia rushed back to his side, gently forcing him to lie back down. "Calm down, sweetie. It'll be okay."

He shook his head. "I don't want to go back. I hate school and I love being with Daddy. Please, Mom, please don't make me go back!"

Alicia closed her eyes and shook her head. "We can't just run away from our problems, sweetie."

"Really?" Trav said from behind her, a bite in his voice she'd never heard before. "Seems like that's exactly what you're doing."

She turned to look at him, but he was already gone.

CHAPTER FIFTEEN

Trav paced the main floor living room. The three-story view of grass, trees, the river, and his Sessa yacht was lost on him. He'd been so patient the past week and a half—no, the past eight years—trying not to push Alicia. He'd given her time to figure out that they were brilliant together, that Trav loved her and would spoil her for the rest of their lives, but most of all that Preston wanted them to be a family, and dang it, his boy deserved that dream. Trav had never had it. His parents had split when he was two and he'd been shipped back and forth his entire life. The truth was he had very little contact with either of them now. He didn't want that for Preston.

He probably shouldn't have left Preston's room while he was so upset, but he didn't want his son to see him angry like this.

Soft footsteps descended the steps. Trav wanted to stay turned away from her and make her beg his forgiveness or something, but like the wimp he was he turned and stared. Even as mad as he was, he was drawn in by her natural beauty—the light that shone from her eyes, her golden hair, those green eyes that bewitched him. She was wearing a simple tank top dress, and her shape about killed him.

She didn't say anything until she was right in front of him. Trav refused to speak first.

"Can we sit?" she asked, gesturing toward the leather couches.

"I really can't sit right now," he said.

She nodded her understanding and stood facing him.

"Were you going to tell me or just call an Uber in the morning?" he ground out.

"I would've had Preston tell you goodbye."

"And you?"

"I don't know." She shook her head and looked out the windows. "Why do you have to make it so hard?"

"I make it hard?" Trav could not believe she'd just said that. "I've tried to do everything I could to make you feel comfortable and loved."

"Why do you have to make leaving so hard?" She glanced at him from beneath her dark lashes and gnawed at her lip.

"Why do you have to leave?"

"Come on, Trav. We have a life, and so do you. Did you think I was just never going to go home?"

"I hoped." He clenched and unclenched his fist.

Her lips softened and she took a step closer, her soft hand on his arm. "I don't know how to make this work."

"But you want to?" Hope flared in him again. He prayed she wouldn't kill it. He'd been up and down far too much over the past week and a half.

"I ... I'm so confused, Trav."

He gently touched her cheek. She leaned into his touch, and he found the bravery to say, "I love you, Ally. I've always loved you. Please give us a chance."

She smiled, but her lower lip trembled. Trav couldn't resist leaning down and gently kissing those soft lips. Ally sighed and leaned into him. Trav pulled her closer. He wanted to devour her lips and never stop, but he needed her answer even more. "Please," he whispered.

Ally closed her eyes, clinging to his back. Long moments dragged by. He wanted to bring Preston into the discussion—he knew she'd do anything for their son—but this wasn't just about Preston. If Ally didn't love him enough to be with him, he'd somehow have to live with that.

"I love you too, Trav," she admitted.

Trav whooped and swooped her off the floor. He spun her in a circle, then kissed her long and good.

Ally giggled, but sobered much too quickly. "But Preston and I still have to go home, and I have no clue how to reconcile our lives together."

Trav's glee disappeared too, because he knew she had a point. He couldn't just ditch his team, his career, and his life any more than she could forego her responsibilities.

He ran his hands gently up and down her arms. "I know it won't be easy, but isn't what we have together worth trying to figure it all out?"

Alicia framed his face with her hands. "You're the eternal optimist, aren't you?"

"When I'm around you."

"Preston and I have to go home tomorrow, but I don't know why you couldn't come see us soon." She looked almost shy.

He nodded; she was extending the olive branch. "Let me deal with everything here and I'll be there early next week."

She smiled, and it was absolutely exquisite.

"And there's a box with your and Preston's names on it at every race."

"Since when?"

"Every race of my career." When her eyes widened, he pressed his advantage. "Can you make Daytona?"

Daytona was like a thorn in their past that they somehow needed to rip out and cover with salve if this relationship had hope. She swallowed and looked down, but then her back straightened and she met his gaze. "Plan on me being there."

Trav bent down and kissed her, savoring each sensation, her smell, her touch. "I love you, Ally," he whispered against her lips.

"I love you too."

He continued kissing her. They hadn't solved every problem and she hadn't committed to marrying him again, but at least his hopes were still alive and she was in his arms.

CHAPTER SIXTEEN

Alicia had been home a few days, and luckily she'd been busy enough she hadn't been able to fully mourn not having Trav with her every minute. Now that she'd given herself permission to love him, he was all she could think about. They texted often and talked on the phone every opportunity they had. She kept bugging him for when he would make it to Alpine. He was being deliberately vague, but she hoped that it was really soon.

As she drove in from work, Preston ran out to her Maxima to greet her. He'd recovered quickly, just like the doctor said he would. It was such a relief.

"Hey, Mom. Come and eat quick so we can be early for the game. You think I'll be ready to play again by next week?"

"Maybe. You're doing really good. Let's start with practice next Monday, okay?" She was proud that he wanted to go support his team, even if he couldn't play.

A truck pulled into the driveway. Alicia's stomach filled with lead as she realized who it was.

Duke's long legs arrived first, followed by his tall frame encased in Levi's and a T-shirt. He had a really nice build, but it was nothing compared to Trav's. He grinned. "There's the prettiest girl in the West. Why you been avoiding me, sugar?"

She forced a smile. She'd texted him a few times at Trav's house, and since she got home she'd only explained what had happened to Preston and that she was too busy to get together.

"I know this little dude has a game tonight. Why don't you ride with me, then we'll go for ice cream after?" He ruffled Preston's hair.

Preston gave Alicia a pleading look. He'd never really been excited about spending time with Duke, which was fine now that she was going to write the guy off. "Run inside and grab your stuff," Alicia told him. "Wait, I mean, don't run. Walk."

"'Kay." He sauntered off.

"Is he doing good?" Duke asked when the door closed behind Preston.

"Yes, wonderful, thanks."

Duke took a step closer and tilted her chin up with his palm. "What about you? Have you been missing me as much as I've been missing you?"

"Um, Duke, I—"

He cut her off with his lips covering hers. Oh crap, she should've written him goodbye with a text or phone call to avoid this happening. She heard a door shutting. Was Carson here? Oh, he was going to make so much fun of her.

Alicia ducked her head and then had to fight to squirm out of Duke's arms.

"What's going on, sugar?" Duke asked.

"Yeah, I'd like to know that too."

Alicia whirled and squealed, "Trav!"

His face was set and his arms were folded across his chest. She didn't care. Running to him, she wrapped her arms around his back, but he didn't unclench his own from his chest. "Trav, please. This isn't what it looks like."

"Trav?" Duke asked. "Your ex-husband?"

"Daddy!" The front door slammed closed and Preston came hurtling down the steps.

Alicia moved aside as Trav opened his arms and Preston leapt into them. She watched their reunion with tenderness and a leaden stomach. She'd divorced Trav when she saw what she thought were compromising pictures online. He'd seen her being kissed by Duke in real life. Would he forgive her?

Duke stepped up next to her. "Why is your ex-husband here?"

Alicia sighed and tugged at her sleeve. "Well, um ..."

Trav turned to glare at her, the smooth, brown skin of his brow wrinkling. "I've been rearranging my schedule to get here as quick as possible and you haven't even told your boyfriend about me?"

"It's not like that, Trav. I haven't even seen him."

"What's going on?" Duke demanded.

"Well, um, Trav and I ..." She looked to him for help, but his jaw was set and his eyes were angry.

Preston was glaring at her too. Good heavens.

"Can you give us a minute?" she asked Trav and Preston.

Trav's eyebrows went up. He took Preston's hand. "Take all the time you need," he growled.

Oh my, male pride. Yet she knew exactly how he felt. She watched the two of them stomp into the house before she turned to Duke. "I'm sorry, Duke. I didn't want to tell you like this, but I love Trav and we're trying to work things out."

"What?" He swept his cowboy hat off and pushed a hand through his hair. "When did all this happen?"

"On the cruise," she said miserably. Duke was a really nice guy and she was a jerk treating him like this.

"Wow. I thought he cheated on you and you couldn't be married to a race car driver."

She wrapped her arms around herself. "Well, um, all of that happened a long time ago and ..."

Duke studied her with hooded eyes. "You're just going to push that under the rug. Why? For Preston?"

Alicia shook her head. "There's a lot going on. Trav never cheated, I think, and I ... I love him."

"Sounds like you still have a lot of questions."

"I do, but I have to give him a chance. He's my son's father."

He sat there for a few seconds. Then his mouth twisted like he'd eaten a lemon. "He's going to hurt you again, Alicia. He's the same guy who only wants to race cars, not be part of your and Preston's lives. He's never even made it to a hockey game. What does that say? Can you guarantee he'll put you first?"

She had no response to that. How could you guarantee that someone wouldn't hurt you? She thought she knew Trav so well, but they'd never discussed the tabloid pictures and the fact that Holly was still part of his life. She'd love to move past all of that and figure out how they were going to make it work, but as mad as he probably was at her right now, it was going to be tough.

Duke wrapped her up in a hug, and she took the comfort of it. He'd been a friend and he was a good man. "If things change, you know where to find me." He jammed his hat back on his head and climbed into his truck.

Alicia turned toward the house, but before she could climb the steps, Trav and Preston were there. They were both still scowling at her. Good heavens. This wasn't going to be fun.

"Preston says he has a game to get to," Trav said before she could start apologizing.

She nodded. They walked toward Trav's rented Escalade.

"I'm sorry," she managed when Trav got her door.

"We can talk later. Let's make it about Preston right now."

CHAPTER SEVENTEEN

Trav fumed through the hockey game and ice cream afterwards. He tried to be friendly and charming with all the parents of Preston's friends, many of whom wanted an autograph and were thrilled to meet him, but his gut churned and he couldn't stop picturing Alicia in that tall cowboy's arms. The guy hadn't even known about him? What in the world was Alicia playing at? The ring in his pocket burned. He'd come here thinking he would propose and carry Ally and Preston off into the sunset. What an idiot he was. How many times was she going to rip his heart out and dance on it?

He focused on Preston as his son chattered throughout the game about offensive tactics and how he would've stopped that puck if he was the goalie tonight. He'd missed Preston these past few days and ached for Ally. He'd worked overtime on training for his race and dealing with business with the race company and advertising sponsors so he could get to them as quickly as possible, and his reward was Ally in some other yahoo's arms.

Far too quickly, they were back at Ally's house and he was settling Preston into bed. He really liked Ally's two-story clapboard-sided farm house, built half a mile away from her parents' home on the ranch. The yard and home were well-kept and he wondered if she had any help or worked herself to the bone. Knowing Alicia, it was the latter. He was anxious to talk to her without Preston or that cowboy around, but what was he going to say? What should he say?

"Daddy?" Preston said sleepily when there was a pause in songs. "Are you going to stay here with Mom and me?"

Trav's gut tightened. "I have to get back to train for my next race, bud." He didn't know how much to tell his son about all the obstacles in the way of them being a family.

"Oh." Disappointment filled Preston's voice. "I was hoping you'd be here for my next hockey game. Mom thinks I might be able to play next week."

"What day is it?"

"A week from Saturday."

"Oh. I have a race that next day." Daytona. He'd been so excited to think Alicia and Preston would be there, but this was exactly what Ally had tried to explain to him. They had their own life, and right now he didn't know if it would include him for more than just temporary stops. "I'll try to make the next one, 'kay?"

Preston nodded sleepily. "I'm glad you're here. Love you."

"Love you too." Trav kissed his forehead, then sat there as Preston drifted off to sleep. His son was everything to him and he knew the boy idolized him, but he couldn't even make his hockey game. Had never made a hockey game. What kind of Dad did that make him? The Disneyland Dad. He hated it.

He finally pushed himself to his feet and eased down the stairs. He could hear Alicia in the kitchen stacking dishes. He paused in the doorway as she bent and lifted a stack of plates from the dishwasher. She turned to put them away and saw him. Her back stiffened.

"Hey," she said. "He doing okay?"

"Always. He's a great kid. Thanks for all you've done to raise him."

She arched an eyebrow at him. "Sure. You've been part of it too."

He jammed a hand through his hair. "Not nearly enough."

She gave him a forced smile, then turned and finished unloading and putting away the cups.

He simply watched her. She was so beautiful, but he felt further away from being with her than ever.

When she finished and turned to him, he gestured to the living room. "Can we talk?"

She nodded, walking stiffly in front of him and settling on the couch. Trav sat next to her, clasping his hands together so he didn't reach out and pull her close like he wanted to.

"Trav, I'm sorry about not telling Duke. I really just haven't had time."

"So you were kissing him to tell him goodbye?" Sadly, he couldn't keep the bite from his voice.

"He kissed me, not the other way around." Her green eyes flashed at him.

"Hmm, that sounds suspiciously like what happened eight years ago when you claimed I cheated on you with Holly."

Now her eyes were sparking fire. "Oh, you want to bring Holly up again? That's perfect, because we've never had a chance to hash out why you not only cheated with her, but never fired her."

"Why would I fire her? I never did anything wrong with her."

"Says you."

"Yeah, says me, and sadly, if you can't trust that, I'm not sure we have any future together."

Alicia closed her eyes and turned away from him. "Maybe you're right. When I think about you and her together I get a knot in my throat that threatens to choke me."

He eyed her. She really did believe he'd cheated on her. "I don't know how to prove I never cheated on you, and honestly, it ticks me off that you can't just believe me."

"Well, honestly, it ticks me off that she's been by your side the past eight years."

Trav blew out a breath. Maybe he should've fired Holly to prove his devotion to Alicia, but would it have helped? "She's been a fabulous assistant and never crossed any boundaries since that day she tried to kiss me and the press took all those pictures of us." He lowered his tone. "But if I would've known it would help you trust me, I would've fired her on the spot. I still will."

Alicia regarded him for a few seconds, then shook her head. "Even if Holly and Duke were a nonissue, what then? Are you going to give up your lifestyle? Or do you think it would be good for Preston if we chased you around the country?" She sighed heavily. "I can't make either idea work in my brain, Trav."

Trav pushed to his feet. "So that's it? Either I give up racing or I never have my family?"

She withered into the couch. "I don't know, Trav. I would love to say that I could just follow you around, but there's Preston, my mom, the ranch, my career. I can't just dump everything to be there for you, no matter if I want to or not."

He paced in front of her for a minute. "I don't know how to get past this, Ally. Seeing you with Duke ripped me up, but I understand that isn't the real problem." He shoved a hand through her hair. "I love you and Preston, and you know what hit me tonight?"

"What?"

"I've never even seen my boy play hockey. I've missed out on so much, but ... you know me, Ally. Racing is who I am. How do I leave that?"

"That's why I've never asked you to." She brushed a tear away.

Trav sank onto the couch next to her and wrapped his arm around her. "Oh, Ally. Don't cry."

"Sorry. It's just so hard. I love you too, but I don't know how to make us work."

"Unless you're okay with a dysfunctional lifestyle of me flying here every chance I get and you and Preston coming to see me when I can't get away. Then I have almost a full two months off in December and January." He tried for a cocky smirk but failed.

"Oh, Trav." Alicia buried her head in his chest and didn't answer him. It was probably for the best. They were a mess and he didn't have any way to fix it. Unless he gave up racing altogether.

CHAPTER EIGHTEEN

Trav stayed for two days, but they didn't spend any time alone. It was a Saturday and Sunday, so they could both focus on Preston and try to push away the reality of their situation.

Monday morning he was supposed to fly out to prepare for his race next weekend. Alicia had an eight o'clock meeting with a client. She dressed in a fitted jacket and pencil skirt then rushed down the stairs, kissed Preston and hurried for the door.

Trav was blocking it. "Whoa there, darlin', you gonna leave for work without a kiss?"

"Wouldn't dream of it, cowboy." Alicia couldn't help but smile as he gathered her into his arms and gave her a kiss she would remember for a long time. Her lips tingled and her hair was messed up when he finished.

"Sheesh, Dad," Preston moaned.

"You're okay running him to school before you go to the airport?" she asked to avoid the bigger issues.

"Yes, ma'am." He still held her close. "I'm going to miss you."

"When are we going to see you again?"

"Aren't you coming to Daytona this weekend?"

"Um, I don't know. Preston has that hockey game and I don't know if we can get a late flight ..." She trailed off at the frustration in his eyes.

"But you said you would."

"I know. It's just so hard."

He released her and pushed a hand through his hair. "I understand." His voice said he understood too well. Daytona was when they'd really blown apart. Even without the hockey excuse, she didn't know if she could handle it. "I'll try to come back out in a few weeks," he said. "Maybe during the middle of the week if my trainer will give me a break."

"Okay." She smiled bravely and gave him a quick peck on the lips, like they were a couple and she was just going to work and he would go to his day job and they'd be all normal and together.

"Bye, Mom," Preston called when she pulled the door open.

"Love you, buddy. Have a great day." She gave Trav one more nod, then hurried out the door. She couldn't prolong this goodbye; it was painful enough knowing this odd relationship would never last. One weekend in and they'd already had a blowup about Duke and Holly, and he felt guilty for not being to Preston's games and she felt horrid for not knowing how to support him in the career he was born to do.

He followed her out onto the porch, and she knew the memory of his face drawn into a frown would be with her for a long time.

CHAPTER NINETEEN

Trav was almost ready to climb into his car. He felt the adrenaline rush he always got before a race. His crew chief slapped his shoulder. "You're gonna take this one, boss."

"Thanks, Jay. I have a good feeling."

Jay grinned. They said the same lines before every race. Superstition, good luck, whatever you wanted to call it.

Trav made a quick phone call, nervous to even ask. "Are they here?"

"No. Sorry, Trav." Holly's voice was heavy with disappointment. She'd been working all day to make his box perfect, filled with all the pictures of Preston, Alicia, and him from their cruise, and stocked with every food and flower Alicia had ever suggested she liked. After the race, he was going to propose to her and they were going to make their crazy relationship work. Other drivers did it; why not him?

He'd texted her last night and explained that he had a private charter waiting for them in Jackson after the hockey game. He had confirmation that she and Preston had gotten on it from the pilot, and from her text teasing him about not taking no for an answer. He'd replied that he wasn't going to take no from her ever again. He'd had such hope, but why wasn't she here? Could she really not handle watching him race, or was it just because it was Daytona?

He pocketed his phone and slid into his car. Jay looked concerned, so Trav forced a smile. "Don't worry, friend. I've got this."

He sat patiently through the harness and mic checks, then jerked his helmet on and gunned the engine. *I've got this.* That was a lie. He didn't have anything. Where was his family? Why couldn't Ally be here for him? He forced all thoughts from his mind as he said a quick prayer and pulled onto the track. He was racing, and it was what he was born to do.

The limo that came for Alicia and Preston at their hotel on Daytona Beach was five minutes late, and then they hit traffic. She wanted to get out and run. Would the race start and Trav wouldn't even know she'd been there? She wanted to be there for him, to make this work somehow. That's what you did when you loved someone, even if it was hard and broke your heart in the process. She could text him that they were on their way, but she wanted it to be perfect. A text picture of her and Preston in his booth would be ideal but she'd settle for the parking lot at this point.

Preston fidgeted in the seat next to her. "Are we gonna be late, Mom?"

"Maybe." She hugged him. "Sorry."

"I hate missing the first of the race," he muttered.

They finally pulled into the parking lot and the driver let them off out front. Alicia heard the boom of the announcer's voice—"Gentlemen, start your engines!"—then the roar of the cars. They'd missed it. She so wanted Trav to race knowing she was there and that she loved him.

The limo driver must've paged someone, because there was a nice older gentleman who directed them to an elevator and took them up to the top of the stadium. He walked them to a booth and opened the door, gesturing them inside.

Alicia looked out the bank of windows at the view of the racetrack, her eyes searching, searching ... there he was. Number 88. He was near the front of the pack. That was good. He hadn't told her how he'd done in qualifying, but he looked to be starting around ninth.

"He's looking good," Preston exclaimed.

They walked together to the front of the large box, their eyes glued to the racetrack. Alicia could smell flowers and food, but she wanted to focus on Trav not investigate right now.

"You're here," a woman's voice said from the side.

"Hey, Holly!" Preston called out happily.

She rushed over and gave him a hug, then looked at Alicia. "He was so hoping you'd come."

Why did she have to be here? This moment belonged to Alicia, Trav, and Preston. She believed now that Trav hadn't initiated the contact that the tabloids alluded to, but he'd still kept Holly around all these years and it was just awkward.

Holly gestured to the side table. "He had me order all your favorites."

"It smells really good ..." Her voice trailed off as she saw the bouquets of spring flowers and the pictures on the walls and the tables. "Oh, Trav."

Everywhere she looked there were pictures of her, Trav, and Preston on the cruise. Even some of them at the dolphin encounter, at the fort, and their other day trips. Her eyes flew back to Holly, who gave her a hesitant smile. Alicia tried to return it before checking on Trav's position on the track. He was in fifth now. Her heart was in her throat. Trav was so thoughtful and she loved him, and it was harder than she'd imagined watching him fly around the track. She could still picture her dad's car slamming into the wall. The flames. The pressure in her chest and scratchiness of her throat. Then the news that he was gone. She shook her head. She couldn't do this right now.

She looked at Holly again. "Thank you for all of this." She gestured around. If Holly felt anything for Trav, this had to be hard.

"He loves you so much."

Alicia's stomach was taking flight. She focused back on the race. Preston was glued to the window, watching his dad maneuver into the number four position. She wished she could see Trav, talk to him, hold him.

"I need to tell you something," Holly whispered.

Alicia looked over, surprised to see the woman right by her side.

"I made the pass at Trav all those years ago. I was infatuated with him and thought we were meant to be. I'm sorry."

Alicia said nothing, her throat too thick. Trav had told her the same thing.

"When the tabloids insinuated a relationship between us, I was ecstatic. He tried to fire me, but I gave him my sob story about how I was raising my sister and needed the job." She smiled sadly. "That is actually the truth. Then I worked my butt off the past eight years so he wouldn't want to fire me."

Alicia stayed focused on the race, but she had to ask, "So when I came here eight years ago ...?"

"I lied to you that he'd cheated with me and told me he loved me, and then lied to him that you were never here. I'm very sorry."

Alicia's gaze snapped up. She should probably accept the apology, but she could hardly believe Holly had blatantly lied to her and to Trav and waited this long to tell her. Trav didn't know that she'd come here. "But why ... you lied, and now you're finally telling me?"

"I'm very sorry." Holly wrapped her arms around her midsection and studied the racers far below. "I thought for quite a while that I did love Trav, but he made it clear that you were the one for him. Then a year ago I fell in love, for real this time, and I realized if anyone took Rob away from me I would hunt them down and kill them. I justified that you weren't worthy of Trav because you left and didn't support him, but as much as he loves you, I think you two deserve a chance."

Alicia focused back on the racetrack, shocked by the admission, but yet so very happy for the reconfirmation that Trav had never betrayed her emotionally or physically.

"Daddy's in third!" Preston hollered. "I love him, I love him, I love him." He jumped up and down in his excitement.

"Sweet, buddy." Alicia pulled him close, still processing everything that Holly had revealed. She couldn't wait to hug Trav and tell him that yes, it was going to be hard to make their family work, but they loved each other and it was going to be worth all the effort.

She studied Trav's car, love bursting through her heart, but then the old fears of watching him race reappeared. He was going so fast, probably over two hundred miles per hour, and with the drivers maneuvering so close to each other, she could hardly breathe through the worry. She'd always been nervous watching her dad and then watching Trav, until her dad died and every fear multiplied a hundred times over.

"Thank you for telling me," she murmured to Holly, her throat thick with emotion and regret and a little bit of shock.

"Sorry it took me so long."

There wasn't really anything to say to that because hiding something like this for eight years was horrible, but Alicia had a rush of sympathy for Holly. It had to be hard for her too, and maybe it was all the way it should be. Maybe it had taken Alicia all these years to be ready. To watch Trav race, even if she was terrified. To love him, even if their lives were insane and they were apart more than they were together.

They stood there in silence, watching the race. Trav maneuvered around the car in third.

"He's on the move!" Preston hollered. "Go, Daddy, go!"

Alicia smiled, remembering watching her dad race and cheering for him. The excitement of the race rushed through her. The roar of the cars. The cheers of the crowd. She'd missed it. Yes, she was scared, but maybe this was in her blood as much as it was in Trav's and in her dad's. She could never excuse her dad's treatment of her mom, but she'd still been his little girl and loved him desperately. Being back here, it brought all that love back and she said a silent prayer of gratitude that her dad had loved her, despite the mistakes he'd made.

"He's going for it!" Preston yelled.

Trav was passing the number two and number one cars, who were neck and neck. He was going around both of them down low on the left. Alicia gasped and placed a hand to her mouth. "Go, baby, go," she whispered as Preston cheered and Holly started screaming in excitement as well.

He was almost around the leaders. Alicia released her mouth and screamed. "Yes! He's going to take them!"

The car next to Trav clipped his back tire with its front end.

"No!" Alicia screamed, watching in horror as Trav's car spun around the other two and toward the wall. It slammed into the wall, flames shooting out from under the hood. She couldn't do anything but cry out as the vehicle crumpled around him.

"Daddy!" Preston screamed.

"No," Alicia whimpered. Her stomach plunged and sweat broke out on her forehead. Trav. Was he injured? Dead?

Preston turned to her and buried his head in her stomach. Alicia held him close, but she had no words of comfort.

The other cars streamed around Trav, the caution flag slowing them down. The stadium had gone deathly still. It was like everyone sensed what Alicia had always feared: Trav had wrecked, and he wasn't okay.

The red flag was flying now and the cars slowed to a stop so the medics could get to Trav. Alicia stood frozen as they brought jaws of life and started cutting the race car away. Had Trav somehow survived in that pile of hot metal? His suit and helmet would protect him, to a point. Chills overtook her. Nothing had protected her dad.

"Let's get you down there," Holly said. Alicia had forgotten the other woman was even there.

"Okay," Alicia agreed. She wanted to be there, even if the worst had happened. Preston said nothing, simply clinging to her hand as they rode down the elevator to the pits. Within a few seconds, Holly had bossed enough people around that a golf cart came and picked the three of them up.

Alicia held Preston close as they went through a tunnel, then came out on the infield of the racetrack, going around motor homes and right onto the green of the Daytona lettering.

"Take us up to his car," Holly demanded.

"I'm sorry, ma'am. I can't do that even for the wife." He glanced back at Alicia and Preston. "I'll get you as close as I can." He pulled to a stop directly below the wreckage. The firefighters and medics were still cutting away at the car. Did it usually take this long?

Alicia climbed from the cart.

"Is he dead, Momma?" Preston whimpered.

"No, no, sweetie. Your daddy is so strong—" Her voice broke, unable to finish the lie. Her daddy had been strong too. She bent down and looked Preston in the eye. "I don't know if he's okay, love." She couldn't bring herself to say dead. "But I promise I'll be here for you no matter what, and your daddy loves you no matter what."

Tears raced down her cheeks. If Trav was gone, wouldn't there be a disruption in the universe? Wouldn't she sense it?

She gave Preston a fierce hug, then released him. "Stay with Holly."

"No, Momma," he protested, but she pulled away and hurried toward the blacktop.

The firefighters pulled the driver's side of the car completely off and then backed away. Alicia stumbled onto the track, even as someone yelled at her that she needed to stay back.

Trav climbed out of the wreckage. His red overalls were smudged with black. He pulled his helmet off. He looked exhausted and in pain and absolutely wonderful.

"Trav!" she screamed louder than she'd ever screamed in her life. She took off running toward him, ignoring everyone's protests.

"Ally!" Trav didn't run, but he hobbled down the slope toward her, a bright smile splitting his face.

The track was slanted so much, she felt like she was fighting uphill. Trav hurried down the blacktop, reaching her and wrapping her up in his arms. He stunk like smoke and sweat and she'd never been so happy to be in his arms.

"You're okay?" she asked.

"I am now." He grinned and kissed her. Around them, she could hear the crowd cheers, almost deafening, and then the roar of race cars. "We'd better move, love."

They walked together off the racetrack, arm in arm. Holly had been holding Preston back on the grassy stretch, but he broke free when they got close and tackled his dad, about knocking him down.

"I was so scared," Preston admitted.

"Me too." Trav held them both close. "When I hit that wall, I thought I might never see the two of you again."

There was so much Alicia wanted to say to him, but she settled for the bottom line. "Racing is who you are, Trav. I'll support you in that until you're ready to be done."

"I'm ready to be done, Ally. I want to retire to Wyoming, raise my boy, and make more babies with the woman I love."

"Are you sure?"

He nodded as the other race cars poured past them in a deafening roar. "I'll miss it," Trav shouted to be heard, "but you and Preston are much more important."

The medics had followed them off the track. They escorted Trav to the ambulance so they could check him out. Alicia wanted to discuss everything in more detail later, when he hadn't just been in a life-threatening accident. She kissed him before the paramedics pulled him away. "I love you, and you look really hot in overalls."

He chuckled. "I love you, and you look hot in that pink bikini. Kauai next week?"

She pushed his shoulder, then felt bad when he grimaced. "Kauai any time, love."

He was still grinning when they closed the ambulance doors.

CHAPTER TWENTY

They were back in the booth at the top of the Daytona Speedway. It wasn't hard to get special permission to use after hours if you were Trav Poulsen. Holly and her boyfriend had taken Preston for ice cream and then to a movie, giving Trav and Alicia some much-needed time alone. He'd been released with a clean bill of health a couple of hours after the race had ended. Bumps, bruises, and scrapes, things that would all heal.

Alicia glanced around at all the pictures, stopping at one of her, Trav, and Preston posing with the dolphin—all tan and smiles.

"Thank you for all of this." She gestured around. "I love it."

He pulled her in tight against his chest. He'd been able to shower, and he smelled like his usual musk and man. Oh, how she craved his smell. "I just love you," he murmured. He kissed her softly on the lips.

"I love you." Alicia hated to do it, but she pulled back and rushed out the words. "Trav, I don't want you to come to any rash decisions. Racing is in my blood as much as it's in yours. I hated, hated, hated watching you crash tonight. I knew I would become a shriveled old woman without you, but I don't want to take all of this away from you. It's part of you, you know?"

"It is." Trav nodded. "But you know the best part, Ally? You love me enough to support me and you've never asked me to quit."

She swallowed and forced a smile. She would be here for him no matter what.

"But I truly feel like it's my time. I was protected by angels in that car, Ally. I almost felt like your dad was there, and all I could hear was this voice in my head, I think it was my voice, screaming, *Please Lord, don't make me leave them.* Then it hit me that's a pretty stupid request when I risk my life every week." He held her close. "I love you enough to stop racing. It's been a great ride, but I want to grow old with you, Ally."

This time, Alicia's tears were happy and grateful. She would support him if he wanted to race, even if he changed his mind and wanted to return. Right now he was talking from a huge scare experience, but she knew his love for her was genuine and would always be there.

Trav pulled back slightly and took a ring box from his pocket. Alicia's heart thumped faster. She gazed into his dark eyes, hoping against hope that it was her ring, not something new. She wanted the ring he'd bought for her all those years ago. He gave her a cocky grin. "I always knew you'd come back to me."

She laughed and pushed at his shoulder. "It's the confidence that I love."

"For sure." But his fingers trembled slightly as he popped open the lid. She resisted teasing him about it. "I've held on to this ring for eight long years, Ally. It's always been you, only you." He lifted the box open and her perfect wedding band sparkled up at her. It was a simple white gold band that wrapped up to a two-karat princess cut diamond. Trav gently slid it on her finger. "Alicia June Noir. Would you marry me, again?"

Alicia threw her arms around his neck. Tears streamed down her cheeks as she kissed him, and the wonderful taste of his minty breath intermingled with the salt from her tears. "Yes!"

He hugged her tight and kissed her over and over again. The only thing that could ever top this perfect moment was when they would tell Preston that they were truly a family again.

ABOUT THE AUTHOR

Cami is a part-time author, part-time exercise consultant, part-time housekeeper, full-time wife, and overtime mother of four adorable boys. Sleep and relaxation are fond memories. She's never been happier.

Sign up for Cami's newsletter to receive a free ebook copy of *The Feisty One: A Billionaire Bride Pact Romance* and information about new releases, discounts, and promotions here.

Read on for a sneak peek of *Cozumel Escape: A Billionaire Beach Romance*.

www.camichecketts.com
cami@camichecketts.com

EXCERPT FROM COZUMEL ESCAPE

Brooks Hoffman whistled as he walked along the touristy marketplace of Cozumel. It was a beautiful eighty degrees with a slight breeze coming off the ocean, and since there wasn't a cruise ship in town today, the market was a bit quieter than usual. That meant fewer women, but there were sacrifices he was willing to make for a peaceful shopping trip before Christmas.

He'd already found toys for Zack and Maddie's three children, but he wanted to find something pretty for Maddie, and he had no clue what to buy Zack. His closest friend was taking his family to New York for the holidays to be with his parents. If Brooks wanted to give them presents, he'd have to be ready when he went to visit them on their island for Thanksgiving weekend.

A gorgeous, pint-sized blonde breezed in front of him, tossing him an intriguing smile, her blue eyes sparkling. She ducked into a women's clothing shop before he could turn on the charm.

What was that little dream doing on his island? No cruise ships in port meant she was staying for a week or beyond. Dare he hope she was here for longer than a week? He tsked at himself. He'd never dated any woman longer than a week, so what did it matter? His grin grew.

This one was intriguing enough that it might take longer than a week to tire of her.

He followed her light scent into the women's shop. Apparently, this was the place Maddie would receive her Christmas present from this year.

"Can I help you?" the young attendant called out while folding a cobalt-blue shirt. She glanced up and smiled at him. "Ah. Señor Hoffman. So good to see you, sir."

"You as well." Most of the island knew Brooks by name. He hired a lot of locals, and they'd become his close friends. What could he say? This was his kingdom. Of course they revered him.

He glanced around for the woman. She was in the back, sifting through long dresses on a rack. He sidled his way up to her, bent down, and murmured, "The blue would match your eyes beautifully."

She jumped and took a swing at him.

Brooks stepped back quickly to avoid getting smacked by the woman. She was so small he could bench-press her without raising his heart rate, but her punch had been quick and sure.

"Oh, sorry!" Her cheeks reddened. *How intriguing, a woman that blushed easily.* "I didn't hear you approach, and all of a sudden you're, like, whispering in my ear."

Brooks arched an eyebrow. He liked the way she talked—blunt, and with a Southern accent that could drive a man to buy unnecessary jewelry.

"How in the world did you sneak up on me? You're stinking huge!"

"Training." He was never going to elaborate. "So, South Carolina? Maybe Georgia?"

"Alabama."

"Ah. I like it. Here for a week, or can I persuade you to stay longer?" He winked, and she blushed again. *Ah, innocence.* It could never be bested in his opinion.

"I live here." Her lips turned down and she brushed by him. "If you'll excuse me."

Brooks reached out and gently gripped her arm. She glared down at his fingers, then up at him. How could a woman this interesting live here and he not know about it?

"I don't know if I can excuse you." He took his voice to the depth he knew drove women crazy. "I haven't seen eyes that brilliantly blue in years and find myself quite drawn to you. Dinner tonight?"

"No, but thanks all the same for the invite," she said, with just the right amount of sauce in her voice, like Southern barbecue—sweet and tangy.

"You can thank me later," he murmured.

Those blue eyes snapped up at him, and her pretty pink lips puckered as if she'd licked the salt off of a margarita. Hmm. Salt, margaritas, and her lips. He liked it.

She tugged her arm back, and he released her because he was a gentleman first and foremost. As a child, he'd seen too many men take advantage of women. That would never be him.

She speed walked to the front of the shop. Luckily for both of them, he was quick as a panther. "At least tell me where you're staying. If you're lucky enough, I could convince you to have drinks with me."

She whirled, and her eyes went up his body, down, and up again. Brooks flexed his arms slightly, certain she would like what she saw. A man doesn't spend hours in the gym every day for his health.

Tilting her head to the side, she let that luscious blonde hair spill over her toned and tanned shoulder. He looked forward to an opportunity to pick her up and kiss her until she begged for more. Ah. His life was good.

"I don't drink."

"Oh? Dinner then." He dusted his hands off. It was settled. "When and where shall I pick you up?"

She took a step closer to him, and he couldn't hide a smile of triumph. She'd come around quickly. They always did.

"You can come have dinner with us. I believe our cook is whipping up somethin' special tonight." That accent was being applied thick as frosting. "Tortillas and beans."

Tortillas and beans? Was she kidding? Any child on the island could make tortillas and beans. "Hmm? Yes, while that does sound appetizing ..." She was appetizing, but her dinner offer definitely was not. Yet, it was an opportunity to spend time with her. Sometimes good food had to be sacrificed to woo said lady. "Where is this dinner to be held?"

"Bethel Orphanage. You might've heard of it, just a half mile inland from here." She whirled and stomped from the store.

Brooks's jaw unhinged. Sheer terror rushed through him at the idea of setting foot in the building. The orphanage? He donated vast amounts of money to that orphanage, but had never made it past the wooden front door. The memories of hunger and pain would crash around him, and someone might find out that the mighty Brooks Hoffman was simply a scared little boy who had buried his past rather than deal with it.

"Are you going to go?" The smooth-skinned shopkeeper was by his side.

Brooks pasted his confident smile back on. "Ah, no. I've had enough tortillas and beans to last me a lifetime." He threw his shoulders back and strutted out of the shop before she asked any more questions.

***

I hope you enjoyed the first chapter of Brook's story. To continue reading click here.

ALSO BY CAMI CHECKETS

Rescued by Love: Park City Firefighter Romance

Reluctant Rescue: Park City Firefighter Romance

The Resilient One: Billionaire Bride Pact Romance

The Feisty One: Billionaire Bride Pact Romance

The Independent One: Billionaire Bride Pact Romance

The Protective One: Billionaire Bride Pact Romance

The Faithful One: Billionaire Bride Pact Romance

The Daring One: Billionaire Bride Pact Romance

Pass Interference: A Last Play Romance

How to Love a Dog's Best Friend

Oh, Come On, Be Faithful

Shadows in the Curtain: Billionaire Beach Romance

Caribbean Rescue: Billionaire Beach Romance

Cozumel Escape: Billionaire Beach Romance

Cancun Getaway: Billionaire Beach Romance

Protect This

Blog This

Redeem This

The Broken Path

Dead Running

Dying to Run

Running Home

Full Court Devotion: Christmas in Snow Valley

A Touch of Love: Summer in Snow Valley

Running from the Cowboy: Spring in Snow Valley